# Sturgeon's Case Files XI:
## The Halloween Caper

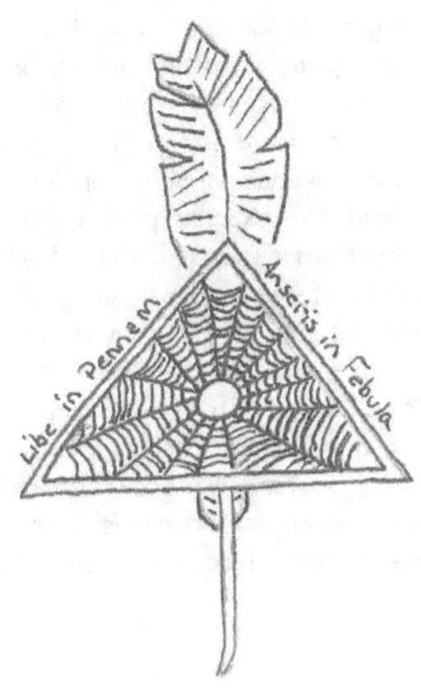


William L. Jeffers

Sturgeon's Case Files XI
Published in The United States of America
By Kindle Direct Publishing
ISBN: 9798373807623
Copyright 2023 By William L. Jeffers

# Jerry Lee Mayes
## 02/17/1947-10/27/2022

We reserve the phrase "Farewell" for the strongest and most meaningful of bonds in life, but for your departure there are no words. There is only a sense of loss. A sense of loss not only for ourselves, our children, our children's children, but for the world as a whole for not knowing you as we did. You brightened the life of all around you unintentionally and without effort. Your wife, daughters, would be sons will mourn your loss, but it is the world that is missing out.

1.
Sunday 13:02

Suzanne enters the home of her boyfriend Dean Warren with her long blonde hair in a single braided rope down her back. Her white floral dress falls to her ankles revealing her white high-heel slippers. She holds her handbag in her hands as Dean walks past her. His slick black hair is in a fashionable wave to the left side of his head. His white button-down shirt is untucked from his plain denim jeans, a fresh buff has been applied to his black leather boots. He sets his truck keys on a narrow table just inside the door of his two-story house that has been Suzanne's home since her house had been burned down only a year prior. Aunt Francis eases past them with her violet walker held close to her body. Her long silver mane falls to the small of her back in curls, Suzanne towering a good three feet over her as she walks past her niece.

Suzanne offers to help her aunt remove the black hand-knitted sweater she wears over her baby blue dress. Laughing softly, Aunt Francis eases one arm at a time off while using her other hand to hold fast onto the walker with their bibles in the seat. They talk casually about the morning's service. Then of the early lunch they had shared at the Malt Shop with Suzanne's brother Sam, Dean, Abby, Dreama, and Abby's husband Darrel. It had been a lovely time, even though the interior dining area of the Malt Shop was particularly crowded and noisy. The pair had been living with Dean, who has insisted since day one that they make themselves at home, but Suzanne had been working tentatively to earn the money to continue the rebuilding of their house.

It has been several years since Suzanne started her private detective business. She looks back occasionally to the day she had found the corpse of a woman in the woods behind her house and decided to help with the investigation to help her brother move towards taking over the Sheriff's position. Sheriff Klinestiver had been over the hill and needed to be replaced long enough that solving the crime had been far more than enough to earn him the elected position. Since that day, Suzanne has made a reputation for herself as a private eye, solving crimes not only in their hometown of Darlington County, Ohio but in the tristate and even in the Amish Country while on vacation. Her brother, Sam, has made a name for himself in his own right as Sheriff by keeping crime rates down and making the community feel much safer.

Keeping to her aunt's rules while living with Dean, she and Dean keep separate bedrooms while not married and Aunt Francis kept her bedroom in the spare study downstairs since she was no longer able to use the stairs. Suzanne and Dean would share company until bedtime but also keep it appropriate. They have been dating for several years and had been engaged for several months before Suzanne was able to let Dean know she was not quite ready for marriage. He had been a perfect, understanding gentleman when he found out and offered to stay in her comfort zone until she was ready.

Suzanne sighs audibly before making her way through the living room to the kitchen where she sets a family-sized package of large chicken breasts out on the counter from the refrigerator. Washing her hands in the kitchen sink, she pulls a large Tupperware bowl from the cabinet along with some barbeque sauces, seasonings, and baster. She empties the package of chicken into the bowl before adding the sauce and seasonings. She smiles as Dean sneaks up behind her and wraps his arms around her waist.

"No hanky panky in the kitchen, children." Aunt Francis warns as she takes her usual seat at the dining table. "Dean, will you put some coffee on, please?" She asks with a sigh, Dean walks over to where she is fumbling with her oxygen tank, taking the hose from her hands and placing them around her ears with the hose ports in her nose. He gently turns the valve connected to the tank, allowing the oxygen to flow freely.

"I sure will, Aunt Francis." Dean smiles as she squeezes his hand. He moves off to the counter closest to the sliding glass doors to the back deck where he keeps his Bunn coffee pot. In a matter of minutes, there is a fresh pot of coffee filling the air with an aromatic Brazilian scent.

With dinner marinating, Suzanne makes her way to her room to change out of her Sunday School clothes. Entering the fascinatingly warm and vibrant room Dean had chosen for her, she walks to the wardrobe where her tee shirts, button-downs, spaghetti straps, and jeans are hung in a color-coordinated fashion. Removing her dress to reveal a white spaghetti strap crop top and blue boy shorts, Suzanne pulls a black Led Zeppelin tee-shirt on before slipping into a pair of tennis shoes and heading from the room. Stopping briefly at the sight of her backpack containing her detective's tools, she slides her cell phone into the back of her shorts before opening the door and heading downstairs.

Suzanne arrives at the bottom of the steps to find Dean at the entry with an older woman in a parka and black leather muck boots. Her skin is a pale whitish-tan color, her eyes covered with sunglasses, and a thick layer of red lipstick covering her lips. She leans on a black and purple metal folding cane, a broad-brimmed black hat with a yellow ribbon wrapping around the brim. She stands about chest level with Dean who is maybe a head taller than Suzanne herself.

"My dear lad, I was assured that Miss Sturgeon was living at this residence." The older woman remarks in a high-pitched voice.

"As I said, Mrs. Tuttle. She does live here, but she is not accepting job offers at the moment." Dean assures her in a slightly louder tone than Suzanne feels necessary. "She is on break from work."

"Well, wake her up." The older Mrs. Tuttle demands as she stops the end of her cane down on the floor. "This is important."

"Ma'am. Please speak to Sheriff Sturgeon for help. He will be more than happy to assist you." Dean advises the woman while Suzanne remains hidden in the bend of the stairs.

"The sheriff's department can't help me, young man." Mrs. Tuttle remarks stubbornly. "Their job is to stop crime, not aid in it." She adds in a hushed tone she mistakes as a whisper but is audible in the confines of the living room.

"Excuse me?" Suzanne remarks subconsciously. "How do you mean, aid in crime?" She inquires as she descends the remainder of the stairs to come to stand beside Dean.

"Are YOU miss Sturgeon, miss?" The older woman inquires impatiently.

"Yes, I am. Now, please, explain?" Suzanne remarks sternly. "It is not my habit of breaking the law either."

"Please, deary." The elderly woman begins laughing to the point of coughing into her fist. She pulls a handkerchief from her pocket to wipe her mouth and blow her nose. "You are notorious for breaking the law to benefit your work." Suzanne blushes at the bluntness and truthfulness of her words. She crosses her arms under her chest and cocks one hip spunkily to the right.

"What is your case?" Suzanne inquires bitterly. "We can start there."

"I smell coffee." Mrs. Tuttle observes with a crooked smile. "Can we discuss it while sitting with a cup of coffee?" She insists as she leans to look around them both into the kitchen where they can hear Aunt Francis humming Hymnal songs. Suzanne looks at Dean with a Tell-Tell expression.

"You two have a seat in here, I will go bring coffee and cakes in here to you." Dean offers as he clasps his hands together in front of him. Suzanne nods thankfully as she holds her hand out inviting the woman to come around the couch to have a seat.

"Thank you, dear." Mrs. Tuttle replies as she scoots around the couch on her feet slowly. Suzanne notices, as she watches the woman making her way around the sofa, that the elderly woman is in her pink house slippers beneath her long black skirt.

"If you don't mind, how about you tell me about the case you have in mind while we wait for Dean to return." Suzanne insists as she takes her seat in the deep brown leather recliner she favors in the sitting room. Mrs. Tuttle chooses the wooden wicker rocking chair Dean's mother had left him when his parents moved to Chicago recently.

"Well, Miss Suzanne. It is funny you should ask." Mrs. Tuttle remarks as she pulls a pack of Pall Mall cigarettes from her purse just as Dean returns to the sitting room with the plate of coffee cakes and two steaming cups of coffee. He is about to protest when she lights the cigarette and pulls the rubber tree from the corner to use as an ashtray. "I need you to break into the old asylum to find my husband, Ashton." Mrs. Tuttle remarks, cutting Dean off as he tries to protest her smoking. She flips the ashes into the wicker pot of the rubber tree.

"Why is your husband in an asylum that has been shut down for over fifty years?" Suzanne inquires curiously.

"Well, you see, he died there in the sixties." Mrs. Tuttle replies as she watches Suzanne cross her legs underneath where she is sitting and lean in with mounting curiosity.

"Then, what makes you think he is there, Ma'am?" Dean asks as his own protests turn curious.

"I have been receiving messages and requests from him." The woman replies while reaching into her purse to pull out a small notebook. Dean sets the tray with their coffee and cakes on the coffee table before taking the notebook and handing it to Suzanne. He takes a seat on the sofa just within reach of the two women.

Suzanne looks at her with her head down looking at the notebook. The notes are written in frantic cursive, but legible. She reads it for several minutes while leaning against the chair backing and flipping through the pages. Her eyes widen and narrow, back and forth as she quickly leafs through the notes of Mrs. Tuttle retelling the accounts of her discussions with her deceased husband. At one point, she lays the notebook open in her lap and pulls out her cell phone. Typing an inquiry into the search engine, she scans through the results until she finds one that suits her desires. Mrs.

Tuttle and Dean sit in anxious anticipation while watching Suzanne curiously.

"What do you think, Suzanne?" Dean inquires impatiently after several minutes of watching her read an article on her phone. His voice draws her from her deep thoughts, causing her to drop her phone into her lap on top of the notebook. She startles and turns to look at him with a surprised expression. "Yes, Suzanne, I am still here." He offers with a broad toothy smile. "What are your thoughts?"

"The claims seem legit, if not a little bit questionable." Suzanne remarks as she holds the blue composition notebook up and waves it in the air for dramatic effect. "Can I hold onto this during the course of the investigation?" Suzanne asks with a gleam in her eyes Dean has not seen for a long while.

"If it helps, deary." Mrs. Tuttle replies before taking another drag from her cigarette and flipping the ashes into the base of the rubber tree.

"Secondly, I won't have to break into the asylum, they do overnight haunting tours." Suzanne remarks with a broad smile. She bites her lower lip, becoming giddy as she leaps from her seat for her backpack. She pulls out her dusty ledger, flipping to the last page that had been written.

"What will you charge me for your services?" Mrs. Tuttle inquires quizzically. "Money is of no concern if you can get to the bottom of this."

"I will require three hundred up front and another four on completion. The results will be worth the price, I assure you." Suzanne informs her as she raises her gaze to meet that of Mrs. Tuttle. Mrs. Tuttle reaches into her purse and pulls out a crumpled and tethered checkbook. She licks her finger and turns to a clear, blank check with an ink pen in hand.

"I'm sorry," Suzanne whispers with a cringe. "I don't accept checks any longer. I was burned last time I did."

"Oh." Mrs. Tuttle remarks with concern as she closes her checkbook and places it back into her purse. "I can go to the bank in the morning and bring you the money afterward. How is noon?" Mrs. Tuttle asks hopefully.

"Noon is perfect," Suzanne replies with a renewed vigor. "I will be waiting for your visit." Mrs. Tuttle reaches into the leafy green moss made of foam and puts her cigarette out before standing from her chair. Suzanne meets her across the floor, placing her arm under the elderly woman's arm to escort her out. Dean sips on his coffee, watching the pair make their way towards the front door while talking and making plans for meeting the following day.

"I can meet you at the Malt Shop at noon if that works, ma'am." Suzanne offers.

"That will be wonderful, deary." Mrs. Tuttle remarks as Suzanne opens the door for her. "I will see you at noon. Enjoy your evening." She tips the front of her broad hat before walking out of the door. Suzanne watches her approach a black Oldsmobile Sedan where a man in a tux with sunglasses awaits her arrival at the back driver's door. As soon as Mrs. Tuttle approaches, he opens the door for her and closes it once she is safely inside. Suzanne ponders the arrangement for several minutes as she watches them pull away from the curb in front of Dean's home.

"That entire interaction was very suspicious," Dean remarks as soon as Suzanne closes the front door and turns to face him.

"There is an insane amount of weird involved in this case already," Suzanne admits with a sheepish shrug. "But, I think that is what is drawing me into it."

"Are you CERTAIN taking this case is a wise move?" Dean inquires with great concern for Suzanne. "I know it will be the largest case you have taken since you took down the crime syndicate, but is it really the case that takes you back out into the job?" He has already stood from his seat to meet her behind the couch in the entryway into the dining room. She takes her by the hands, kissing them one and then the other before kissing her lips gently.

"I thought about that too, Dean," Suzanne admits with a sigh after returning the kiss. "But, it is now or never and this case seems to be just the

amount of weird and suspicious I need."
She remarks with a beaming smile.

## 2.
### Sunday 17:25

As Suzanne finishes preparing the fried barbeque chicken, Dean and Sam enter the dining area to the delight of Aunt Francis. Suzanne rushes to give Sam a hug, this being only the second occasion Sam has been over for dinner since the untimely retreat of his ex-wife Cassie after her abrupt desire to separate and get a divorce. She wraps her arms around him in a loving, compassionate embrace. Sam gratefully hugs her back with his chin resting on her right shoulder. He and Dean are followed into the dining room by Aunt Bee, their mam'maw Patti, Darlington Counties own father Jerry, and Sissy Hannah. Suzanne sets extra places at the table before removing the biscuits from the oven. With dinner ready, they fix their plates and gather around the table where Jerry says grace as they hold hands.

"Dean tells me you have finally taken a large case," Jerry remarks as he reaches for a chicken breast. "I have always been proud of all you kids."

"Yes, so long as she shows up with the first installment tomorrow," Suzanne replies over the butter dish. She spreads a large helping onto her biscuit before continuing her statement. "I will be seeking her late husband in the asylum in Rio."

"Does she truly believe her husband is in that terrible place?" Alannia inquires while waiting for the gravy boat for her mashed potatoes.

"She has a list of documented requests he has made. Each seems as unlikely as another." Suzanne replies with a shrug. "It is a most curious case, and I am looking forward to the work. Plus, the price I named will supply the next month's materials for my house."

"How far along are they in restoring the family home?" Jerry inquires with renewed interest. He passes the gravy boat to Bee while looking to Suzanne for a reply.

"They have finished the foundation and shell of the house." Suzanne offers quietly. "They have laid the floors and outer wall. As soon as I pay them the next installment, they will add electrical wiring, switches, and outlets. Then we will work towards installation." Suzanne informs the table with a glance of despair. They have been a year working towards rebuilding the family home with Suzanne paying for the majority of the labor and supplies while Sam dealt with his failing relationship. Despite her most valiant attempts at supporting the rebuilding, work has been slow, and so has the income needed for the company they had hired.

"That is better progress than none, Dear." Aunt Francis offers as she holds her fork in the air with a tethered strip of chicken dangling from the bent spokes. She smiles a toothless grin, forgetting to have put her false teeth in before dinner. The others at the table begin laughing, breaking the awkward silence that had fallen in the gloom of Suzanne's despair over the slow progress of her home. Despite the circumstances that have plagued the siblings over the past year, Sam and Suzanne find themselves both laughing along.

The remainder of the evening goes well with much conversation and laughter.

The family remains at the dinner table sipping on either coffee or a variety of soda well after they have finished dinner. Jerry pulls his sugar tester from the pocket of his blazer while Hannah stealthily takes the plate of sweets he had placed in front of himself.Suzanne stands just after dusk to collect the dishes along with Dean's help. They carry them to the kitchen sink with Dean resting his left hand on her lower back as they walk. Suzanne can not help but smile after the events of the day and the uplifting dinner visit of family. Bee joins them shortly, offering to help with the dishes allowing Dean to join Sam and Jerry on the porch for gentleman-like talk. Dean offers Suzanne a kiss, one she accepts joyfully, before leaving the kitchen in the hands of Suzanne and Bee.

"He is quite the handsome young man, Suzanne." Bee remarks as she pushes her cheetah print glasses up on her nose. Her short Bob haircut sways back and forth over the collar of her tan shirt and cheetah print cloth bibs. The brown and silver tint of her hair reflects the light from over the window behind the sink. From the window, they overlook the back patio and in-ground pool in the backyard. The back corner of the connected garage is just in view with the outer edge of the back property fenced in and overgrown with trees and wildflowers.

"I am more concerned with Sam," Suzanne admits in a low whisper as she looks over her shoulder to see her brother and Dean walking out of the front door to the porch. "He and Cassie had their problems, by no means did they have a good relationship, but he still saw it through until she left him. Then her parents took over everything as far as getting her belongings or seeking recompense Cassie didn't deserve. He didn't even get to keep the muscle car he saved years for. She managed to take it somehow."

"Suzanne, your brother is strong. Stronger than most." Bee assures her with a hand on Suzanne's shoulder. "No one doubts he will rise from everything he has been through over the past year and be stronger for it."

"I know." Suzanne remarks with a slight tear running down her cheek. "I just wish I would have had him with me the past year rather than him being consumed with his own life. I know that is selfish, but I could have used him."

"You needed one another." Bee corrects her sternly. "The two of you divided when you should have held hands and helped one another through what the other was struggling with. Now, after everything has already done its damage, you have to regroup and reconnect. Maybe you could include him in the case you are taking on and use it to bond." Bee suggests placing both hands in the soapy dishwater. She begins washing plates, handing them one at a time to Suzanne for rinsing and drying.

"I will," Suzanne mutters. She resents the feeling of inferiority and weakness. Especially with a relative, one she sees as a mother telling her that she needs her brother when she has spent so much time strengthening herself and building her own independence. "I will talk to him about it after the dishes are finished."

The pair continue their task until the dishes are all washed, dried, and put away. Suzanne wipes the counter and stove down while Bee wanders over to join Aunt Francis and Sissy Hannah. When Suzanne is finished in the kitchen, she retrieves a pitcher of tea from the fridge and five glasses. Making her way into the dining room, she joins the women at the table, pouring them each a glass before taking her own seat. Patti comes from the restroom with her white hair in a bun on the crown of her head, her sunflower gown held aloft in her right hand. She uses her left hand to guide her strides with a long wooden shepherd's hook cane. Once she is seated again, she sighs deeply while leaning back on the chair.

"Are you about ready to head home, Mam'maw?" Bee asks Patti with a concerned tone.

"No, Margarette. I just ate too much." Patti replies in her usual tone of exhaustion, calling Bee once more by her mother's name.

"Mam'maw Patti, you can lay in my bed if you like." Suzanne offers kindly as she pours a glass of sweet tea.

"I will be alright, sweety," Patti replies with a smile. "It ain't often I get to visit anymore. Bee thinks I need to stay at home all of the time."

"Well, enjoy your visit. I am going to join Dean and Sam on the porch. I need to talk to them anyhow." Suzanne remarks as she stands from the table and excuses herself. Suzanne exits the house to find her brother and Dean leaning against the porch posts talking about the current Darlington County High football team. Dean and Sam had both played, though Sam preferred basketball over football. Suzanne wanders over and finds her place under Dean's left arm with her right arm around his waist.

"The boys beat Mercer last weekend by three points in overtime." Sam is remarking while checking his phone. The dusk to dawn lights are glowing along the street with a mass of small bugs fluttering around and the occasional bat passing through for its nightly dinner.

"I hear the Edmunds boy plowed one of their receivers, taking out a few cheerleaders on the sidelines as well." Dean offers with a chuckle. "I didn't get to make it to the game, I was pulling an all-nighter at the garage trying to finish a job ahead of time so I could work a few more in. I have been doing it so often here of late."

"I haven't been able to return to work yet. James is still filling in for me." Sam admits sheepishly. "I am not sure when I will return to work."

"How about you take another week or two off and help me with this case I am taking on, Sam?" Suzanne offers with a high-pitched tone of uncertainty. "We can do the overnight tour while investigating the appearances of ghosts and looking for Mr. Tuttle."

"It wouldn't hurt to take a little extra time off," Sam mutters while stubbing his toe on the underside of the porch railing. "It is paid time off at any rate."

"Well, I am meeting Mrs. Tuttle at the Malt Shop at noon tomorrow. Want to meet me there about half-past eleven?"

Suzanne suggests casually. She is preoccupied with nestling deeper under Dean's arm as the cool autumn breeze picks up, swooning around them.

Sam agrees to meet her the following day at the arranged time. After entering the house to bid everyone good night, he walks past Dean and Suzanne on his way to his Blazer. After a few minutes, Sam turns his headlights on and pulls from the curb, leaving the lane where Dean's home is located. Suzanne ushers Dean over to the porch swing where they cuddle for the better part of an hour before their guests eventually leave abruptly. With the night growing older, they eventually head in to spend a couple of hours talking before going to their rooms for the night.

Before leaving, Jerry turns and kisses Suzanne on the cheek with a warm smile. She gives him a long, warm-hearted hug finding comfort in his embrace. He does not bother to pull away while Alannia waits patiently on the porch.

"You know, Suzanne," He whispers in his soft yet wise voice. "You can do anything you set your mind to." He reminds her encouragingly with a second kiss to her forehead. "You have the wisdom and strength in you to do anything, great things. You always have. You have followed your own path since you took your first step and let others know they can rely on you. A time will come when you will have to let yourself rely on others, and that is not a bad thing. For the time being, there is not an ounce of weakness in you. Don't let your head fall, keep your chin held high, and know there are no obstacles in your way that you can not endure. I love you, Suzanne. Never forget it." He kisses her cheek once more before releasing his hold on her. His waft white and silver hair fluttering in the breeze. His cheeks rosy and his smile kind. "I'll see you soon."

Suzanne smiles as she watches him to his truck, a sense of overwhelming warmth filling her chest as she leans on the door frame. Time slows to a crawl as she thinks of all the wisdom he has given her. With warm thoughts, she waves to Jerry, Alannia, and Hannah as they back from the driveway.

Suzanne enters her room and closes the door behind her. She begins to walk past the chair that rests by the door holding her backpack and gear securely. After a second thought, she grabs her backpack by the arm strap, the weight of the pack coming back quickly as she guides it over to the bed. She empties the contents one piece at a time, placing her camera and other objects on charge around the room to ensure they are all at full capacity. She flips through the ledger to find it is nearly full with a photo of her and Jerry hunting tucked away in the back. Nibbling her lower lip, she decides to fill it fully but also buy another the following day. She pulls her lockbox from the bag and unlocks it to see what she has remaining as far as finances. Checking a few bank bags and envelopes, she finds she had money she had forgotten about. Gleefully, she texts Dean, telling him what all she found in her work bag. With the new revelation, she asks him to contact the contractors in the coming day and inform them they may progress as planned, and the funds are available.

With all of her equipment charging, she lays out a pair of denim jeans, a black Pink tee, and a Darlington Wildcat hoodie on the dresser for the following day. She places her wallet, keys, and other personal items alongside her clothing and digs out her muck boots. After putting everything away that does not require charging, she loosens the braid in her hair only to brush it out and braid it once more. She lays her hair snuggly over her right shoulder while texting Dreama. She decides to invite her very good if not best friend along with her and Sam to ease the tension on this particular adventure. The fact that Dreama loves anything haunting-related helps her make the decision easily. Once she is ready for bed, she dresses down to only her thin-strapped shirt and boy shorts before crawling under the blankets and turning out the bedside lamp.

### 3.

Monday 11:15 am

Suzanne sits in the driver's seat of her fifty-six Chevy step side baby blue pickup. The shifter is set in neutral with the parking brake set allowing the engine to run for the sake of the heater. Suzanne sits in her Wildcat hoodie, her bag in the truck seat next to her with the main compartment open. She has her old ledger in her lap, open to a blank page, with the new one she just purchased earlier this morning secured in her bag. She looks around the busy streets of Darlington County while parked along the curb opposite the front entrance of the Malt Shop. The rectangular diner with a pale yellow upper half over a deep blue lower is filled with regular and new customers. It is the center of social life in Darlington County.

Suzanne can see the black steel fenced-off court behind the Malt Shop where visitors dine during warmer months along with an open area for dancing. From across the street, she can hear the outside loudspeakers, the volume has been taken down a few notches yet still audible, playing a selection of today's more popular music. She smiles as she jots down a few notes of occurrences during the day leading up to the meeting. Glancing towards the double glass doors entering the Malt Shop, she can see Sam pulling along the curb to the side of the diner, placing his late-model El Camino in the parking space before climbing out into the street. Shutting her truck off and placing it in gear, Suzanne climbs from her truck with her backpack in hand.

Suzanne meets Sam at the entrance to the Malt Shop with her backpack hanging on her shoulders, her right hand placing her phone in her back pocket opposite her wallet. Sam smiles broadly with his fluffy black beard freshly washed and brushed, his dark hair parted to the right side. Suzanne is relieved to see him cleaned up more than he had been the evening before. With a flare of chivalry, he opens the door for Suzanne and steps aside for her to enter ahead of him. Suzanne bows slightly while laughing and enters the diner to make her way to the counter where the last of a line of visitors have just placed an order for a young couple. Suzanne approaches, nodding to the familiar gentleman behind the counter.

"My my, Suzanne Sturgeon. It has been a good minute since we have seen you." The youthful fry cook exclaims audibly from behind the counter. His blue suede shirt and white apron cover the rotund belly of the young man. His cheerful pudgy face and short kempt blonde hair give him the nickname ShowTime.

"It has been a few days, ShowTime. Do I still get the frequent diner's discount?" Suzanne jests as she leans on the counter to look into the kitchen. She is familiar with most of the crew from her regular visits to the diner.

"If we had such a thing, you would be the first on the list." ShowTime remarks with a chuckle. "What can I get you?"

"I will have....a basket of chili cheese fries, two of your double burgers, and a strawberry milkshake for myself. My brother will have the bacon cheddar curly fries, buffalo wings, and a vanilla shake." Suzanne orders carefully while reading the menu as if she has not memorized the menu over the course of previous years. "And can we have another order of hot wings each?" She adds with a smile while watching ShowTime jot down the order with a nod to each item. She pulls her wallet from her back pocket as he rings the order up, handing him a twenty and a ten to cover the twenty-eight dollar and fifty-nine cents cost. He reaches her the change which she places in the tip jar along with a few loose ones she had in her wallet. ShowTime hands her a placard with the number Seventy-one for her to hang on the end of their table before turning to hang the order on a revolving wheel over the stove.

Suzanne makes her way through the crowded dining room to a table in the back corner where her brother is waiting. Suzanne takes the seat in the corner looking over the dining room, hanging her backpack on the seat next to her, she sits with her right leg underneath her and her left knee up with the heel of her foot on the seat. She pulls out her ledger and voice recorder from her backpack getting them prepared ahead of time. Sam hangs his coat on the back of his seat before sitting against the back wall. He watches as Suzanne places the private eye badge he had given her as the Sheriff of Darlington County on her belt.

"I didn't know you still had that," Sam remarks curiously while leaning back in his seat.

"I would never let it go," Suzanne replies casually with a sincere smile. "I am very fond of it. I wear it proudly."

"So you should. You earned it rightly." Sam compliments her with a broad grin.

"Sam," Suzanne addresses her brother with a tone of seriousness. "I know she robbed you of emotion, time, and energy, but you need to move on," Suzanne remarks coldly. She does not mean to come across as mean or emotionless, but she wants to get her point across. "It has been nearly a year. She is not worth wasting more time or energy mourning when your career, family, and friends are worried so much about you."

4.

Monday 12:25 pm

Sitting back in their chairs with their feet propped in opposite chairs, Suzanne and Sam sit restlessly in the corner of the Malt Shop. Their empty trays rest on the table in front of them with crumbled wrappers, empty tray-like cardboard baskets and empty glass milkshake glasses with straws bent over the glass rim. Suzanne is on her phone sending a text while Sam is impatiently watching the clock on the wall over the counter where Showtime is laughing while talking to a young colored woman with long braids down her back. She is wearing a short cropped denim coat over a black tank top and denim shorts. Show time catches Sam looking at her several times, offering Sam a wink in response.

"Sis, it is nearly half past noon and your client has yet to appear. Do you think we are being stood up?" Sam remarks as Showtime points Sam out to the young woman. Sam turns to Suzanne quickly, engaging in conversation while trying to avoid the woman's gaze from the corner of his eye.

"She is old." Suzanne reminds him casually without looking up from her phone. "She is allotted a gracious untimely late arrival. Especially if she is bringing me three-hundred dollars." Suzanne remarks as she shifts in her seat. A boot knife makes a brief appearance inside her left boot. Catching Sam looking at it, she quickly fixes her pants leg over the boot and returns to sitting back in her chair, her gaze still locked on him waiting for him to comment. Deciding to ignore what he had seen, he continues to engage her in conversation.

"How long should we wait?" Sam inquires, not realizing Suzanne is watching the door behind him.

"Just a moment longer, the time it takes her to sit down," Suzanne advises as she lowers her feet from the chair where they have been resting. Sam turns to see the elder Mrs. Tuttle come walking down through the tables where patrons sit eating and talking. Her white hair is in a large afro with a black veil pinned in, flowing over her face. She is wearing a long black gown with shimmering silver worked into the fabric. Her grim mourning appearance draws the attention of all of the patrons, bringing a quietness to the diner aside from the pop music being played over the loudspeaker.

Mrs. Tuttle approaches the table where Sam and Suzanne are seated with her flamboyantly colored handbag hanging from the crook of her right elbow. Sam and Suzanne both stand as she reaches the table, her horn rimmed glasses slipping slightly down her sharp nose. Suzanne walks around the table to the next seat from where she sits to pull the chair out for the elderly woman. Mrs. Tuttle smiles, taking the seat as Suzanne slides the seat underneath her. Sam and Suzanne return to their seats.

"It is a pleasure to see you again, Mrs. Tuttle." Suzanne greets her with a beaming smile. She busies herself preparing her voice recorder, ledger, and pen while Mrs. Tuttle becomes comfortable. "Can I get you something to eat?" She offers kindly.

"No, Thank you." Mrs. Tuttle replies in a somewhat shaken voice. "I have news. My husband contacted me again last night while I was preparing my clothing for today." Mrs. Tuttle informs them in a barely audible whisper of fear.

"What did he want?" Suzanne asks, becoming fully engaged.

"He wishes me to make a sizable donation to a charity he supported before he passed away. Some organization that is known as Drive Gallia." Mrs. Tuttle replies curiously. "I had never heard of it before last night."

"What amount does he wish you to donate?" Suzanne inquires curiously as she begins to write in her ledger. "Does he appear to you visually or only audibly?" She adds suspiciously before continuing to question her. "Does anything curious or bizarre happen prior to or after his appearance? Do you hear any vehicles outside your home on each occasion or an odd light shining in your room? Do you normally see him on the first floor of your home, are there multiple floors." She looks up to see Mrs. Tuttle becoming overwhelmed by her frantic line of questioning.

"I am Sorry, Mrs. Tuttle," Sam remarks casually. "My sister is very....energetic and driven when it comes to her mysteries." Sam apologizes as he holds a hand in the air for a waitress. "Answer in your own time." A young high school girl approaches the table in a pink top and a mini skirt, knee-length white socks, and loafers. Sam orders the three of them each a strawberry milkshake, handing the woman fifteen dollars and advising her to keep the change.

"My room is on the third floor, dear." Mrs. Tuttle offers in a quizzical, quivering tone. "Almost always at ten in the evening. He appears visually and audibly, surrounded in a sort of dull yellow light that seems to be coming from the moon itself." Tuttle describes the circumstances of her husband's visits. "I have not noticed any odd vehicles or pedestrians on the streets. I am usually too enthralled with his visit to notice such things."

"When and where does he want you to make the donation?" Suzanne inquires, ignoring the fact Mrs. Tuttle did not offer the amount that is to be donated. She decides that, at the moment, it is none of her business.

"I am to make the donation this Wednesday at the Bank of Darlington County under the curator's account." Mrs. Tuttle replies meekly. "A Mr. Franklin Marks from Galla district of Darlington County." Suzanne tries to think for a moment. The name seems familiar from a previous encounter in Galla back when it was a county of its own. Unable to place it, she continues with her questioning.

"Is it a great amount?" Suzanne asks again, deciding it may be of some use.

"Thirty-five grand, along with the gem collection he had been saving from his time overseas during the war." Mrs. Tuttle replies while sitting firm and upright. The waitress returns with the three milkshakes, setting one in front of each of the occupants at the table. "I promised to make the deposit into the safety deposit box as requested."

"The next overnight visit at the asylum is tonight. So, with your initial payment, my brother and I will spend the night there to see what we can find." Suzanne mutters while finishing her notes.

"Yes, the three-hundred dollar deposit, the remaining four-hundred on completion." Mrs. Tuttle repeats the agreement as she opens her handbag to pull an orange and blue envelope from within. "As promised, here you are." Suzanne takes the envelope from her hand, opening it to count the contents before closing the envelope and placing it in her backpack's front zipper pouch.

"We will begin tonight," Suzanne assures her with a broad smile. "I assure you, the matter will have our full attention."

"Thank you, Miss Sturgeon. I am pleased to have a detective of your reputation and that of your brother seeing to my affairs. I hope you discern whether or not it is my late husband, and find justice if it is not."

"Rest assured, we will get to the bottom of it." Sam remarks before taking a sip of his milkshake.

Seeing her business concluded, Mrs. Tuttle stands from the table with her untouched milkshake resting on the table where she had been seated. Turning, she walks from the diner without another word. Suzanne finishes her milkshake before reaching for the one left behind by Mrs. Tuttle. Taking a long drink from it, she turns off the voice recorder. She begins putting her things away while Sam merely sits watching her.

"Only you could stumble upon a case like this so close to Halloween," Sam remarks with a smile.

"Sets the perfect tone, does it not?" Suzanne replies with a laugh.

5.

Monday 18:15

(6:15 pm)

Suzanne pulls onto the paved lane leading through an arched gateway in fifteen-foot tall black steel fencing. The paved roadway S-curves along the freshly cut front lawn of the haunted asylum campus adorned with elder palm trees laid out in an unconscious pattern. The asylum is set in the center of the fenced-in campus, rising towards the orange and red dusk sky as an ominous almost sinister entity in the faint light left of the passing day. The dark gray and black shadowing of the already gray brick building appears to hold watchful eyes for the gathering visitors for the night. The building itself is several hundred feet long and almost as many feet wide while towering ten stories, more than one-hundred and fifty feet above the ground with two towers rising from either wing. The center of the structure protrudes from the face of the building leaving dark corners on either side as the face juts twenty feet by twenty feet with solid walls presenting only a double wooden door at the top of a twice counted thirteen steps. Windows on each floor spanning across either wing give the impression that everyone is being watched.

"Well, this place is kinda spooky after all," Suzanne mutters as she follows the winding stone path in her fifties model sleek black sedan. She shifts into a lower gear to decelerate. She peers through the windshield as the asylum grows in her gaze the closer they approach.

"Tell me again, are we going to spend the night exploring this place?" Sam asks reluctantly from the passenger seat. He lifts a bottle of soda to his lips and takes a deep drink before lowering it once more to rest on his left leg.

"It's the first part of the strategy I've laid out for the investigation," Suzanne mutters just as they enter the parking lot. She pulls into a parking space towards the front of the building where half a dozen other vehicles are already parked. Setting the parking brake, she climbs from her car, pressing the locking button. Sam climbs from the passenger door as Suzanne is reaching into the back seat to retrieve her backpack, locking the back door as well. She slips her backpack over her shoulders as they make their way to join the other guests on the sidewalk leading to the entrance of the asylum.

A group leader and event organizer stand in front of the gathering group of five other guests talking to one another in low voices. Suzanne works her way around the group towards them, turning her voice recorder on in the mesh side pocket of her backpack. Suzanne actively approaches while pulling her camera from her backpack, twisting so as to reach within. She droops the camera strap around her neck while standing as close as possible to the two men while trying not to be obvious. She can just pick up the voices with her natural hearing, hoping the voice recorder will pick them up better.

"Where is David?" The taller, more robust male inquires. His wavy brown hair and dark complexion give him a mild appeal despite his obese size. He is wearing a red shirt with a large folding collar and the asylum emblem sewn on the left breast. His khaki shorts have a handheld radio clipped onto the hip pocket and a chained wallet in the right back. His white tennis shoes are scuffed but otherwise clean.

"He has a side hustle during the day. An under-the-table job." The second, leaner and noticeably shorter mane replies. He has short cropped blonde hair with a dark goatee. Wearing the same uniformed clothing, he is holding a clipboard with a pen and a second handheld radio. "He should be here soon, he said he may be a few minutes late today." He adds while lighting a cigarette with his free hand.

"This is the third time this month." The taller man remarks scoldingly. His sense of authority gives Suzanne the impression he is in charge of the event. "Warn him however you like, if this kind of behavior continues he will be fired."

"I'll make sure he knows." The second man concedes. He pulls a cell phone from his back pocket as he walks off a slight distance while dialing a number. Wanting to catch the conversation, Suzanne rushes to the guest nearest where he walks off and tries to engage her in a conversation while trying to eavesdrop on the man's conversation.

"Hello, I am Suzanne." She introduces herself as she reaches the Red-headed young woman dressed in a black cropped top low cut blouse with a short black skirt and black high heel knee length boots. The young woman has at least one half dozen necklaces sporting various gothic medallions while wearing black lipstick and eyeshadow. Suzanne takes a stance placing the voice recorder only a few feet from the shorter attendant.

"A pleasure, I am sure most people would find such a person." The gothic red-head mutters while rolling her eyes. "But why do you think I must know your name?"

"We are both going to be spending the night here. I thought maybe we could get acquainted." Suzanne offers with a shrug. She speaks low, hoping to overhear the conversation going on behind her.

"David, it's Paul. Where are you, man? Dustin is red." He speaks with an exhausted tone. "You need to get here asap. I can't keep covering for you. The old woman has her instructions, so come to work."

"I have no desire to get acquainted with you, ma'am." The gothic red-haired young woman remarks snottily. She holds her hand up to Suzanne to stop any further attempts at conversation and walks away. Suzanne stands awestruck with her lower jaw hanging limp, missing out on the rest of the conversation between Paul and David. When she turns around, Paul is turning around, placing his cell phone back in his pocket, and begins walking back to where Dustin stands waiting.

"He is on his way," Paul announces with a smile. "He is almost here, just ran into some traffic on thirty-five. He said to give him five minutes."

Suzanne leaves her position at the front of the group to join Sam to the left of the attendants. Sam has his hands in his pockets watching the others in the group with a smile and a pleasant demeanor. He seems to be in the midst of a conversation with a pleasant-looking young woman, maybe a year his junior. She has long flowing reddish hair with streaks of black. Her dark-rimmed glasses amplify the size of her eyes threefold. She is wearing a black and yellow tee shirt with butterflies and sunflowers. Her denim knee-length pants have threaded holes on the upper thighs, fitting her complementarity as she cocks one hip. A ring pierces through the bridge of her nose between her nostrils. Suzanne approaches in time to over-hear them poking fun at how the goth girl had spoken to her.

"She was very rude," Suzanne remarks heatedly.

"She was more than rude," Sam's new friend counters with a smirk on her crimson lips.

"Sis, this is Gabbers. Gabbers, my sister Suzanne." Sam introduces them casually while swinging himself side to side at the hips in a somewhat self-entertaining manner.

"You're the private detective from the gas station." Gabbers remarks with a nod of recognition.

"Yep. My boyfriend Dean owns the service station. He let me put my office in the back." Suzanne replies casually while turning her voice recorder off and placing it back in the mesh side pocket of her backpack.

"What brings you and Sam to this asylum? Do you have a case that has something to do with it?" Gabbers inquires, suddenly filled with interest as she looks from Sam to Suzanne.

"Sorry, that is private information," Suzanne mutters while making notes in her ledger. She watches the parking lot while adjusting her camera to take candid photos from chest level so as not to appear suspicious and enabling her to catch photos of individuals. "Just assume we are here for innocent entertainment." She advises her brother's new friend.

"Maybe I can help." Gabbers offers in a hushed whisper. "I like mysteries."

"What do you do for a living?" Sam inquires curiously.

"I am a receptionist," Gabbers admits as she lowers her gaze. "It was the best job I could find after graduating. I have been looking for something better, but jobs are scarce at the moment." She admits sheepishly. Sam looks at Suzanne with a pleading expression causing her to sigh.

"Do you think you can keep close to the attendants during the tour?" Suzanne asks patiently. "I mean within hearing distance.

"Yeah, I can," Gabbers replies with an enthusiastic tone.

"I will help her." Sam offers with a wink. "We can take turns asking questions and keeping them distracted in case you need to fan off from the group to investigate a lead."

"Fair enough," Suzanne mutters while shaking her head from side to side casually. She runs her hand over her camera as a new attendant appears, climbing from his car. He is a rather muscular young man in his late teens or early twenties. He is tan-complected with curly brown hair and flashy jewelry. He approaches, wearing the same uniformed clothing as he passes the gathered visitors to join the other two attendants. Suzanne follows, turning her voice recorder back on.

"Sorry I am late. I got stuck in a work zone on thirty-five." David states with a cheerful tone. "Are we about ready to get started?" He asks while looking around at the visitors. His gaze falls on Suzanne where she stands towards the front of the group. He smiles and winks at her, flashing his perfect white teeth in a broad grin.

"It is a good time to start," Paul replies as he checks his watch. "What do you think, Dustin?"

"Five minutes early, but why not. Let's get this over with." David retorts with a sincere tone of failing interest. Suzanne rushes back to her brother and Gabber, handing them a spare voice recorder.

"It is fully charged and the memory is empty," Suzanne instructs them on how to turn it on and cause it to record quickly. "Keep it recording, it can record up to a straight twenty-four hours. I want to catch everything." She advises them before ushering them to the front of the group with the device already recording.

"Good evening," Dustin calls loudly as he addresses the asylum guests. "Welcome one and all to the West Gate Asylum for the criminally insane." He gestures to the looming structure in the center of the grounds. "The seven of you will be spending the night within its walls, hearing stories and visiting spaces where occupants had once stood. Where they once slept. Where many took their last breaths." He flourishes his words with a broad grin as he continues his monologue.

"I will not lie to you," Dustin adds with a dramatic pause and a deepening drop of his voice. "The asylum is rumored to be haunted. While I will not say for certain one way or the other, odd things have happened. People have gone missing during tours only to be found later with no memories of having ever come here. Descendants of the inmates have been known to have received messages from loved ones beyond the grave. Voices have been heard from the rooms, ghostly images have appeared, and all becomes clearer after dark. So, as we enter the asylum for the night, keep an eye on the person next to you. Look after them, don't split off from the group, and don't panic." Dustin instructs explicitly before turning and leading the group towards the steps leading to the entrance. His two co-workers stay back, waiting to bring up the rear of the group. Suzanne quickly turns her voice recorder on and prepares her camera.

6.
Monday 19:22
(7:22 pm)

Suzanne actively investigates the entrance as she follows in the back of the pack with only the two attendants behind her. She tries to slow her gate to allow them to pass as she looks over the doors, their hinges, and the locking mechanisms. Paul, seeing her falling behind, lingers a moment before urging her to follow the group more closely. Suzanne grumbles with discontent over their watchful presence. She was able to see an extensive amount of fresh scraping around the lock openings indicating someone tampering with the locks. She makes a mental note as she moves to catch up to the others.

In the narrow hall of the entrance, there are numerous doors on either side of the hall. Dustin and the group are gathering towards the first intersection of four hallways. Suzanne gazes at the doors and their corresponding placards as she passes. Most appear to be offices for staff and personnel. Two appear to be the offices of specialist doctors. Suzanne snaps several photos as she passes with plans to research the names once she is back home. One name in particular sticks out, Dr. Svocklian. Suzanne takes a close photo of the name thinking she had heard something about such a doctor in school.

Suzanne catches up to the group, pulling her backpack from her shoulders, and opening it as she approaches Sam and Gabbers. She passes a handheld radio with an earpiece to Sam, keeping it low to his side as she passes it from her hand to his. She places her earpiece in her left ear, clipping her radio to her right hip. She nudges her brother before slipping her backpack back over her shoulders and slipping her way to the back of the group.

"Here we are at the first of many passages in the asylum." Dustin remarks with his arms held in the air. "The east wing was named after the founder of the asylum back in 1808. Jon Anthony was a pioneer in psychology with more than three decades of experience tending to his mother who was afflicted with what we now call schizophrenia. The west wing was then named after his first nurse when she passed away mysteriously at the age of twenty-one during a midnight shift in 1812. It is said, she was found in the basement where they held experimental procedures." Dustin informs them while reading the information from an index card.

"What experiments were they performing in the basement?" Gabbers inquires as she catches a brief moment while Dustin is shifting through cards.

"Electroshock, for starters," Paul replies from the back of the group while Dustin gives an expression of surprise and the abrupt question he was nowhere near ready to answer.

"Soaking in tubs of cold water in their birthday suits." David offers from the other side of the hall from Paul. "That was one of Anthony's favorites."

Suzanne watches the men as they lean against opposing walls with their arms and legs crossed. She looks around the hall in a desperate attempt to find a way to give them the slip. They are currently enthralled by the details Dustin is reciting, finding it very amusing that he was caught off guard by a guest. To her left, she notices a plank of wood hazardously covering what appears to be the broken grate to a vent. It is positioned to the side of a cluster of the guests who are now all throwing questions at Dustin.

Ducking into the shadows of the walls with the guests giving her cover, Suzanne quietly pries the plank of wood free and sets it aside. taking advantage of the clamor of the group, the disgruntled Dustin, and the two amused attendants Suzanne crawls head first into the vent, slipping away from the group.

She finds herself in a stone vent, crawling blindly in the dark, cobweb-filled space with her backpack scraping against the roof. Listening intently, the two attendants seem not to have noticed her disappearance and the other guests are not offering any words about her missing. Smiling, she lays on her belly and pulls a flashlight from the side pocket of her backpack. Switching it on, she can see the tunnel extends for about ten feet before splitting off to the left and right. Suzanne begins to elbow crawl to the junction and peeks in either direction.

Slipping her hand into her left hip pocket, she pulls out a compass to check the direction she should take. The right tunnel leads west while the left appears to run southeast at a slight angle. "Well, now what, Suzanne?" She asks herself timidly. She pulls her backpack off, using the small space to pull out a small notebook, pen, and a large roll of knitting twine. She slips her backpack back on before getting started. Sighing, she writes out notes leading to the first junction of the stone vent works. She finds an anchor on the stone walls where she ties off one end of the twine to leave a trail.

Letting the twine unrivaled behind her, Suzanne takes the southeast passage with her notebook and pen in her back pocket, her flashlight in her right hand. She crawls on her elbows for what seems like an hour before coming to an exit vent or a continuing passage. She looks out into the room with her flashlight to find an examination room. Prying the grate loose, she climbs out into the room with her flashlight fanning out over the room. She ties the twine off to the grate before severing it for further use. She finds several antique instruments a practicing physician would use to examine patients. Most are crude instruments with little or no practical use at all in today's medicine. She searches around for notes or signs of life in the room of late. Finding nothing of any help after about twenty minutes' worth of searching, Suzanne anchors the thread to the leg of a metal table before crawling back into the vent and continuing in the southeastern direction.

Suzanne crawls on her elbows for another twenty minutes before coming to another set of grates on opposite sides of the tunnel from one another. Suzanne forces the grate to her left open first, crawling out into the room to find another examination room. Both rooms are set up for examining patients, neither yielding much information to aid Suzanne in her case. Sighing and dusting cobwebs from her arms, she ties off the twine to the grates before making her way to the door. Using the handheld radio, Suzanne contacts Sam.

"Sam, if you can, respond to me with where you are." She speaks into the radio quietly. She waits for a few minutes for a response before hearing her brother speaking aloud as if talking to someone else.

"Where are we, in the layout of the asylum I mean?" Sam speaks his question clearly.

"The west wing, named after Anna Hemming as previously mentioned." Suzanne can hear Dustin reply to Sam's question with an excited vigor.

"I am in the east wing, investigating examination rooms," Suzanne informs her brother quietly. "Keep them distracted as much as possible. If you hear any important information, relay it to me as soon as possible." She instructs him carefully before opening the door to the room. She enters the hallway with her flashlight leading the way. The wall opposite the door she exits through has a portrait of an older man in his mid-forties. He has eccentrically wild white hair with a large nose and deep hollow eyes. She looks at him for a moment before taking a photo of the portrait.

Suzanne continues to head east along the hall, looking into each room, one after another, finding them all to appear as either examination rooms or supply storage. Suzanne begins to feel defeated with disappointment and dread as she turns a corner in the hall, her flashlight lowered to the floor. She scratches her head before looking up to see the path she is traveling. Stopping dead in her tracks with her light pointed down, she looks into the glowing form of a man in his mid-twenties. His form is transparent with his waving sleeves rustling on the floor, and his baggy sweat-like trousers stained with an unknown substance. Suzanne allows her gaze to peer through the man to the cobblestone floor continuing behind him.

"Oh, snap," Suzanne mutters with wide eyes and a trembling hand.

The ghostly figure turns to look at Suzanne as she mutters her vocal surprise. His brilliant dull yellowish-orange light illuminates the dark gray cobblestones of the walls and floor.

Suzanne backs up towards the opposite wall as he approaches with an expression of curiosity. Suzanne plans a method of escape on the off chance the figure becomes hostile before the thought occurs to interrogate the ghostly figure.

"What...who are you?" She stammers quizzically.

"Are you my love? My Lila?" The figure inquires passionately. "I can not see you dear, but I can hear your voice as if you were right beside me.

"Lila?" Suzanne inquires curiously. "Lila Tuttle?" She adds skeptically.

"It is you. Isn't it, Lil." The figure remarks joyfully. "It's me. Tony. You have come to visit me at last."

"Listen, Mr. Tuttle," Suzanne presses forwards while taking a couple of photos. "Tell me, why did you contact me about depositing in the savings account?" She inquires, deciding to use the confusion of the spirit to her advantage.

"The funds must be deposited so I may pass on to the afterlife." Tuttle urges her with sincere dread. "Otherwise, I will be stuck here indefinitely."

"Why that charity?" Suzanne asks in hopes of throwing Tuttle off. "Why not Darlington 17, the nonprofit group that helps underdeveloped children have a chance to graduate high school and go to college. Can I donate to that charity?"

"I promised the donation to Drive Gallia. I was once friends with the curator Franklin." The spirit explains as he continues to move ever so slowly towards where Suzanne has been standing. Suzanne gives him a wide berth and rushes down the hall behind him about ten feet. "We had a falling out because I did not keep up my end of the bargain, of the business. I owe him the donation."

"The amount you specified is a bit more than I can get my hands on at the moment." She snaps a series of rapid photos before switching her camera to video. "I can do half the amount and half the gems." The spirit of Tony Tuttle turns angrily on the spot to look in the direction of Suzanne's voice. The light around him has taken on more of an orangish-red color as his figure grows twice its size. When he speaks again, his voice is more sinister, deeper with more resonance.

"You will deposit as I have instructed. The full amount by the deadline I have given." His voice roars, filling the hall with the heat and smell of brimstone. The cobblestones seem to collect the heat causing Suzanne to sweat from all of her exposed pores. The dimly lit lights spaced out every ten feet pulse on and off at odd intervals. Suzanne finds herself backing up another ten feet, trying to place distance between her and the ghostly spirit of Tuttle.

"Suzanne," Sam whispers in her ear, nearly catching her by surprise. She finds herself reassured that he was in some ways there with her. "We are preparing to move to the second floor, the private rooms for the more fortunate or more wealthy patients. They are doing a head count though and realize someone is missing. Where are you?"

"I am in the west wing, having a very unpleasant conversation with the late Tony Tuttle.' Suzanne replies quietly. "Cover for me for a bit."

"Look, Tony," Suzanne stutters patiently. "I will pull all I can from our accounts, but I doubt I can get the full amount." Suzanne feigns once more while continuing to back-pedal from the corporeal figure.

"You are what?" Sam comes across the earpiece a little loud, giving Suzanne the impression other members of the group may have overheard him.

The figure of Tony Tuttle roars in rage before lifting from his feet. He lunges at Suzanne rapidly floating through the hall with his arms outstretched. Suzanne turns to run, using the pulsing moments of light to guide her through the hall towards a sharp right, and turns one-hundred feet down the hall. She passes several doors on her right-hand side, running at a speed that does not allow her to examine them in her attempt to get away from the spirit. Tuttle is about to catch up with her when she takes the sharp right, tripping over something she missed two feet into the hall. Falling to all four and rolling to her left side, she looks back just in time to see the transparent figure of Tony Tuttle pass through the stone wall out of sight. The halls go dark for a couple of minutes before the lights return to normal.

Suzanne looks around while breathing deeply. The figure is gone, along with its creepy aura. The lights are back to normal with the heat dissipating along the hall. Sam is talking into her ear, but with the chaos of the past few minutes, her attention is trained on the area where the figure had disappeared. she stands from her position on the floor, dusting herself off before going to examine the wall more closely.

"Suzanne, answer me," Sam demands impatiently.

"The ghost just disappeared angrily into a wall. I am taking a look at it now." She informs whim as she raises her flashlight to look at the wall.

"One of the attendants is coming to look for you." Sam remarks in a whisper. "They overheard you say you are in the west wing."

"How long do I have?" Suzanne inquires while still giving the wall a good once over. She doesn't find anything of particular interest. No trap doors or evidence of it opening in any direction, the wall appears solid. It does however seem to shimmer in a large oval while casting a momentary shadow of Suzanne on the wall before disappearing. Suzanne turns to look for the source of light, finding only the lights on the wall every ten feet.

"About three minutes," Sam replies reluctantly.

"That is two more than I need." Suzanne remarks as she looks down to see another vent grate hidden in the wall. She crouches down to remove the grate and climbs in, pulling it back into place. She ties off a frayed end of the twine before moving east along the back western wall.

## 7.
## Monday 21:35
## (9:35 pm)

Suzanne moves along on her elbows, wiggling along the stone ventilation system with the twine unraveling behind her. She has lost time since entering the vent, seeing only two exits along the way. One entered into a sort of storage room but the grate wouldn't open no matter how hard she tried. The other entered back out into the hall. Suzanne considered it for a moment before hearing someone approach. Laying still with her gaze in the hall, she watched as feet belonging to one of the attendants moved past a few times before lingering in the hall just outside of the wall where she is hidden.

"I haven't found her yet, Dustin." She hears Paul remark. "There is not much of the west wing left to search."

"You have to find her," Dustin growls through the radio in Paul's hand. "I will take the other guests to their break room for the time being and send David to help you."

"Yes, sir," Paul replies. "What are we going to do if we don't find her?"

"We will have to cancel the tour and bring the police in," Dustin replies with a tone of concern. "Then we will all be questioned during the search and the tours will be shut down."

"What if David and I make her disappear permanently? It will only add to the haunting lore." Paul suggests quietly.

"If you can find her without anyone seeing and leaving no mess, go for it," Dustin replies quietly. "Leave no trace though. Dispose of her in the basement." He instructs sternly.

"Yes, sir. Send David, we will get it done." Paul remarks with a joyful tone. Suzanne lays on the vent floor with her hand over her mouth listening intently.

"Do you think the Tuttle woman sent her?" Paul inquires curiously.

"Just stick to the plan. Tony will help find her and send her running right to you." Dustin instructs once more. "Over."

Suzanne lies still for several more minutes listening to the typing of a text on Paul's phone. He stands just outside of the vent, leaning against the opposite wall with his feet crossed. Suzanne thinks for a minute before pulling her cell phone from her back pocket and sending a text to Sam.

"Give me directions to where they are putting all of you. I will meet you there." Suzanne instructs him in a text. It is only a few minutes before Sam comes across the radio and explains where the room on the first floor is where the group is instructed to take a break while they search for her. Using the map online, after pulling it up on her phone, she works her way through the vents until she arrives at the back of the cafeteria. Watching through the vent, she waits until no one is paying attention before removing the grate and exiting the vent quietly. She ties off the twine, cutting it free, and silently replaces the grate while everyone in the room is in a heated discussion as to what had happened to her. They are so caught up in the events of the night, that no one notices her entering the room. Standing, she dusts herself off before finding her brother and Gabbers.

"Did I miss anything good?" Suzanne whispers in Sam's ear as she stands on tiptoe from behind him. Sam turns around in surprise and wraps his arms around her before pulling away and slugging her shoulder gently.

"Hey!" One of the guests calls out in surprise. "She's here!" The goth girl announces in surprise.

"I have been here all along." Suzanne lies with a broad smile.

The guests gather around Suzanne as she takes a seat at one of the pristine white tables added to the asylum when it becomes a sideshow. Dustin breaks his way through the crowd to advance on her. Suzanne looks up at him with a smirk while pulling a fresh bottle of Dr. Pepper from her backpack and taking a generous drink. Sam stands to stand beside her with his right hand on her shoulder. The light in the room is dull, despite the more advanced wiring and accommodations. The dust and cobwebs in Suzanne's hair are hidden when she takes her hair down, placing her hair tie on her wrist.

"Where have you been?" Dustin asks sternly. His glare is more than enough to tug at every one of her nerves after hearing to what extent they planned on making her 'disappear' to help build the sinister reputation of the asylum. She is not certain she did or did not see a ghost, but she is fully aware of the three questionable guides of the tour.

"I have been in the back of the group all along." Suzanne looks him square in the nose with a gaze telling of a knowledge he would rather her not have. "I have been following all along, listening to a podcast over my earbuds. Much more interesting."

"We looked. You had disappeared." Dustin mutters. His appearance transforms from one of authority and sternness to one of uncertainty and concern for self-preservation.

"Sorry, I skipped off to the loo momentarily." Suzanne shrugs. "I couldn't hold it any longer so I found a corner in a room and took care of business." She pulls a half unraveled roll of toilet paper from her backpack and shows it to him. "I was a girl scout at one point. Always prepared." She grins with a twinkle in her eye. Dustin walks away using his radio to call Paul and David back. Suzanne takes another drink of her Dr. Pepper while putting the toilet paper away.

"What did you find out?" Sam inquires while the other guests move away. Gabbers stands right next to him, curious about the siblings and what they have seen thus far. The gothic young woman stands in a corner eyeing Suzanne curiously.

"Not much, yet." Suzanne holds back while making eye contact with the unique goth. "Just circumstantial evidence."

"You're not telling me something," Sam remarks casually as he sits on a seat next to her. "Tell me."

"I met Tony Tuttle." Suzanne offers casually. Her gaze stays joined with the goth girl's, finding her interest curious. Suzanne closes her backpack, placing it on her shoulders as she stands, and makes her way across the room to the corner where the goth girl stands. She ignores the protests and questions Sam is calling after her as she crosses the room with several sets of eyes on her. She approaches the corner of the room where the goth stands with her arms crossed. Turning her back to the adjacent wall only a couple of feet from her, Suzanne leans back on the cold gray stone wall with her arms crossed and her right leg crossed over the left with the hells of her muck boots tilted on the floor.

"I am not sure if you caught my name before. I am Suzanne Sturgeon." Suzanne offers with a smile.

"Angela Miller." The dark and gloomy goth woman introduces herself.

"Find something interesting?" Suzanne inquires sourly. "Find me interesting?"

"A bit. You brought this entire tour to a halt by 'appearing' missing." Angela remarks with a smirk. "No one has seen you, we all know you were missing, but you have us questioning whether or not you were missing," Angela observes.

"Misconceptions or mistakes are a frequent issue in events such as this." Suzanne offers with a yawn.

"But you are Suzanne Sturgeon, I did catch your name. I have followed your career in the tabloids." Angela counters as Dustin prepares the other guests to begin moving again.

"I am on vacation," Suzanne remarks casually.

"No, you have been on vacation for almost a year. You are here on a mystery and I want to tag along." Angela corrects her with a large smile.

"I'll make you a deal." Suzanne offers casually. She pulls a stick pen with a small bead from her hand and offers it to her. "If you can peg one of the guides discreetly with this, you can follow me." Suzanne passes it to her while watching the other guests preparing to leave the cafeteria.

"What is it?" Angela inquires curiously.

"A listening device I can trigger remotely," Suzanne explains. "Ping it to David or Paul preferably. Somewhere where it won't be seen."

"I can do that. Give me just a moment." Angela perks up and crosses the room in a few long strides. Suzanne watches her with mild curiosity as she approaches Paul who seems to smile at her with a broad hormone-driven teen expression. Suzanne watches as she places a hand behind his head and draws him in to whisper in his ear. Suzanne smiles as she witnesses the sleight of her hand. Pressing the earpiece in her free ear, she uses an app on her phone to turn it on. Suzanne blushes as she overhears what Angela is hinting at while still pressing the stick pin bug into his hair. She decides not to mention the exchange when she returns.

Angela kisses Paul's cheek before turning to make her way back to where Suzanne stands waiting with a bashful expression. Without saying a word, Suzanne leads her to the back of the gathering group with Sam and Gabbers at her left side. They give one another an awkward glance as Dustin leads the group of seven guests from the break area. Paul and David bring up the rear, each keeping a closer watch on Suzanne now that they have had to look for her only for her to reappear with the group.  They move from the cafeteria into the dimly lit stone halls a little more than midway along a wide hall. To their right, is a vast hallway of five wooden doors encasing a plexiglass window with black lettered labels. To the left is an intersection with a brass caged lift in the corner of the eastern wall and a set of stairs to the immediate left with the hall continuing another ten feet.

"The lift is not functional, sadly, due to risk management." Dustin chimes in as they gather at the intersection. "I am afraid we will have to take the stairs. Please travel in single file along the right-hand side of the stairs." He instructs pompously as he leads the way up the stairs. Several forms a single file line behind him with Sam then Gabbers, and Angela leading in front of Suzanne. Suzanne brings up the rear with Paul and David following only a few feet behind her. She has her backpack in her arm searching through vaguely while giving off the misconception she is searching for a bottle of soda.

Using sleight of hand, she palms two small rubber balls between her palm and a bottle of Dr. Pepper. Slipping her backpack back over her shoulders, she opens the bottle and takes a swig before nudging Angela. Pointing ahead to the point where the stairs abruptly turn to ascend in the opposite direction with a stone platform joining the two directions. A brass handrail runs on the outside of the steps, giving an iron handhold.

"Have you ever been to the Malt Shop in town?" Suzanne asks Angela casually as she steps up beside her. Paul begins to protest her leaving the single file formation, but Suzanne cuts him off while continuing her conversation with Angela.

"They have the best burgers and curly fries. Plus, their milkshakes are the bomb!" She raises her hands to emphasize her expression, revealing the two balls in the palm of her hand to Angela. Her eyes grow wide as his gaze turns to Suzanne before her intention becomes clear. Once Angela understands, she shakes her head in response.

"No, I've never been," Angela replies curiously as they begin to turn the corner. Suzanne winks at her before throwing the first of the two grenades to the platform at their feet.

Smoke bellows in the stairwell, filling the space with a thick grey veil preventing anyone from being able to see. Suzanne quickly grabs Angela's hand before rushing back down the stairs to the first floor where the smoke begins to clear. She drops the second smoke grenade before pulling them both onto the lift and slinging the lever forward. The lift creaks before slowly shimmering. Suzanne anticipates it lowering into the basement, but it merely shudders and dies. Grumbling, Suzanne grabs Angela by the hand again and rushes off down the hall looking for a door or room they can enter to get out of sight. Behind them, She can hear the disgruntled tones and curses of the others on the stairwell. Turning to her right, she finds a maintenance office. She pulls Angela in and closes the door behind them.

The room has a single narrow wooden desk with only a small wooden rotating chair towards the back wall. There are a couple of coats hanging on hooks just inside the room and a rusting file cabinet rusting against the wall. The light in this room does not flicker on when Angela flips the switch.

"Are we just going to hide in this room now?" Angela asks skeptically.

"No," Suzanne replies as she walks around the desk with her flashlight in her hands listening in on Paul.

"That Sturgeon girl slipped off again." Paul is reporting to Dustin reluctantly.

"You go find her," Dustin replies sternly. "Don't upset the other guests, but take her brother aside and see if he knows where she is and what she is doing. Have David work him over."

"There is usually a maintenance shaft in the maintenance offices that leads from floor to floor," Suzanne informs Angela while searching the back wall. "I am trying to find it. A lot of this is going so much differently than the way I intended."

8.

Monday 23:56

(11:56 pm)

Suzanne searches the back wall before finding a section of the stone that is a false appearance. She pulls it aside to reveal a four-foot by three-foot door hidden in the wall. She reaches for the knob to find a skeleton lock just above the knob. Grumbling, she stands and turns to the desk. One by one, she begins searching the drawers for a key while Angela watches curiously. With no luck in the drawers, she begins searching the filing cabinet and any other hiding places she can find in the small office.

"Dustin must have the key," Suzanne concludes while wiping the sweat from her brow. She pulls her backpack from her shoulders and crouches by the door. Holding the flashlight between her left cheek and shoulder blade, she pulls her lock-picking tools from her back and sets to work. After a mere few moments, she has the door unlocked and swinging open. She puts her tools away with a sense of satisfaction.

"That was....awesome!" Angela exclaims as she rushes to join Suzanne by the small door. "Where did you learn to do that?" She asks curiously.

"I trained myself for months to be able to do it well," Suzanne admits sheepishly as she opens the door to look into the shaft. The shaft is about three feet by three feet with a ladder running vertically on the wall opposite the opening. Suzanne shines her flashlight down the shaft while putting her backpack back on her shoulders. Duck walking, she reaches for the ladder and eases into the shaft. Looking back she winks at Angela.

"Going down." Suzanne smiles as she begins descending. Suzanne climbs with one arm wrapped around the ladder and the flashlight held in her other hand.

She keeps the ladder illuminated for Angela to enter the shaft. They use the light to descend into the darkness with the faint light from the maintenance office quickly fading. They climb slowly in the cramped shaft with sweat rolling from their foreheads and brows into their eyes. Their arms and hands become slippery from perspiration. Cobwebs stick to their bodies and cling to their hair. Their bodies tingle with the spiders and small bugs crawling over their flesh causing them to cringe.

They descend for twenty minutes before coming to a floor of the shaft. Suzanne leaves the ladder first, advising Angela to give her a minute due to a lack of space. She searches briefly before finding the door. Twisting the knob, she finds it locked as well. The keyhole is warped with age, the bronze covered in a coat of rust and decay. Discouraged, Suzanne pulls out her tools knowing she will have to be gentle with the lock in this condition.

Suzanne spends several minutes carefully working on the tumblers in the corroded lock while Angela hangs tiredly on the ladder. At long last, she hears the pins and tumblers pop open allowing the door to swing inward. Suzanne squeezes through giving Angela room to climb from the ladder while shaking her trembling limbs.

The two young women exit the maintenance shaft into a dark room. Only the light from Suzanne's flashlight gives any illumination in the dusty, mold-smelling room. The chill in the chamber feels damp and musty. Suzanne stands from her crouching position to her full height while stepping further into the room. Her light shines across the walls to a closed door adjacent to where she has entered. She finds the only furniture in the room is a flat metallic surface on a shiny metal pedestal. If it were not for the dust and cobwebs, she would think this piece of medical furniture was brand new. It has a pair of stirrups near the footrest with an instrument tray clinging to the side. At least a dozen medical instruments are laying on display on the table. Suzanne examines them closely to find a scalpel, forceps, and a long pair of thin tongs.

Feeling a bit uneasy, she picks up the scalpel, sticking it in her back pocket for defense. Shining her light around the room, she finds Angela standing just inside of the access shaft with her arms crossed over her chest. Nodding her head towards the door, Suzanne leads the way with Angela just behind her. She opens the door slowly, the rusted hinges giving off the sound of a trumpet in the quiet chambers of the basement. Both girls wince physically as Suzanne quickly swings the door open in hopes of rushing the noise. Shining her flashlight forward, they find themselves in a red stone hallway with a white stripe running on either side halfway along the walls. The stripes are cut off only where large metal doors are placed in the walls.

"What kind of rooms are these?" Angela whispers curiously in Suzanne's ears.

"On a whim, I would guess for the hopeless cases or the more violent patients," Suzanne responds in a whisper. "Come on." She eases out into the hallway, creeping along quietly while keeping her awareness active for anything out of place.

Suzanne approaches the first door set into the wall on her left-hand side. Raising herself on tiptoe, she peers through the narrow pane of glass with her flashlight shining in. The window is dusty from the inside and smeared with some thick substance. Discouraged,

Suzanne lowers herself flat-footed again. She searches around the door for a knob, becoming bewildered by a lever set into the stone wall with a green and red glass dome the size of a quarter. The lever is set into the wall as a foot-long shaft of flattened steel at a point along the center of the door. Suzanne tries to raise the lever from the downward position only to find it stuck in place.

"Will you hold this, please?" Suzanne turns to Angela, handing her the flashlight. With Angela holding the light on the lever, Suzanne crouches low, placing both hands on the steel shaft, and begins pushing up with her entire body. Grunting with the strain of determination, the lever suddenly pops free and flips to the upward position. Suzanne stumbles chest first against the lever, nearly tripping over her feet. Both girls wait patiently for something to happen only to be disappointed when the only result is dust and rust particles falling from the pendulum of the lever.

"I wonder if the levers are powered by electricity?" Angela

stammers. "Like flipping a switch." She adds as an example.

"That is a good idea, but we will have to find the breaker," Suzanne replies with a sigh as she takes her flashlight back. She nods down the hall and leads the way quietly. "There should be an office or maintenance room here somewhere."

The two young women travel along the dark corridor with only the dimming light from Suzanne's flashlight giving any light. They pass by numerous doors, both girls losing count after twenty-four, without finding any sign of an office or store room. After about an hour, Suzanne is about to suggest returning to the maintenance hatch when she stumbles onto an intersection at the end of the hall. Directly across from where they stand, an open door presents itself. Suzanne leads the way with her flashlight batteries nearly depleted. She rushes into the room hoping to find something worth her trouble to find the room is an administrator's office.

Suzanne looks around quickly, giving the room a glance over before finding a second door in the back corner. She tries the nob carefully, becoming frustrated when she realizes it is locked. Suzanne once again has Angela hold the light while she pulls her backpack off. She quickly pulls her lockpicking tools out and within moments she has the door open. She nearly jumps for joy when she notices a breaker box in the back of the large closet. Putting her tools away, she retrieves the nearly dead flashlight from Angela's hands and sets to examine the out-of-date breaker box.

With the adjustment of some components and the flipping of a switch, the basement is filled with dim light from the still functioning lighting fixtures. In the distance, they can hear the sound of a large metal door popping open and screeching to a halt.

"Well done, very well done." Angela claps and cheers while bouncing on her tiptoes.

"Now we can have a proper look around." Suzanne sighs as she shuts her flashlight off and places it in her book bag side pocket. "I need to change those batteries." She remarks more to herself in a whisper than anything. She exits the small closet where the breaker box is located back into the office. Watching Angela sit in a swivel chair and begin spinning, Suzanne begins searching the drawers of the desk looking for any sort of clue. She is halfway through the desk drawers when she remembers the cell door that had popped open when she turned the power back on. Standing up straight, she rushes from the office and back down the hall to the now open cell door.

The door to the padded cell is cracked open only a foot when she approaches it with apprehension. She turns to see Angela catching up to her from behind. Moving slowly and carefully, she places her hand on the edge of the door and pulls it open a foot or two more. The yellow padded walls are faded with layers of mold and mildew that have gathered over the years. There is a fluorescent bulb pulsing between light and near darkness statically in the ceiling. The stone floor is covered in filth and dried moldy feces to the back corner where a twinkling catches Suzanne's eye.

Suzanne enters slowly, crouching near the object in the far back corner. Angela stands in the doorway watching her curiously with one hand on the door and the other on the frame. She is preparing to speak when a shadow approaches from behind. With a great shove, Angela is shoved into the room face first onto the cold stone floor. Her flailing body crashes into Suzanne, thrusting her sharply against the wall as the door is slammed closed behind them. Suzanne tries to scramble to her feet in time to rush the door, only to find it already locked. She crashes into the door with enough force to make her stumble backward before approaching the door again. She raises herself on tiptoes to peer out of the window in hopes of seeing who is outside the room.

"Let us out!" Suzanne calls angrily. She slams her fists against the door repeatedly to no avail. "Let us out!" She calls again to an empty hallway.

"What about your radio?" Angela inquires with a frightened tone as she rolls to a sitting position. Suzanne looks at her briefly before pulling her radio from her hip and pressing the key enabling her to transmit her voice.

"Sam. Come in Sam, over," Suzanne growls into the radio while beginning to pace the floor. She waits several minutes with no reply.

"Samuel. Answer me!" She calls desperately into the radio while resting her free hand on her stomach. "I am in trouble and I could really use your help."


******


Sam watches as Paul and David approach Dustin, whispering to him with urgent expressions. Looking around, his hand reaches instinctively to the radio clipped inside of his left hip pocket. Gabbers grabs his hand, preventing him from raising it just as the three attendants gaze through the guests looking for any sort of reaction or discomfort.

"They are trying to see if your sister is here with anyone." Gabbers remarks while subconsciously holding his hand comfortingly in hers.

"Something is wrong," Sam remarks impatiently. "She has not contacted me for a good while."

"You said she is dedicated to her investigations." Gabbers reminds him cheerfully. "Could she just be lost in her work? Plus, she has that other girl with her."

"I would like to say this is out of character," Sam admits as the three attendants separate. Two retake their places in the back of the group while Dustin remains in the lead. "Truth be told, this is right up her alley. Still, I need to check on her." Sam whispers as he hooks his thumbs in his pockets in an effort to press the communication button on his radio. He can hear the static that accompanies the process allowing him to transmit his voice. With a steadily growing discomfort, he speaks lowly over the voice of Dustin describing sections of the asylum.

"Suzanne. Are you there Suzanne?" Sam asks quickly. "Respond if you are able. Use Morse Code if in trouble." He instructs carefully. He waits for several minutes while following the group with growing anticipation. When there is no reply, he transmits another message eagerly for a response. When his message goes unanswered again, he turns to Gabbers with an expression of concern. Turning to look at the back of the group, he can see Paul and David watching the members of the group, and for a brief moment, he makes eye contact with Paul before making a rapid decision.

Sam passes through the two other guests between himself and Paul to approach him with a feigned bashfulness. Gabbers, curious as to what he is planning, places her arm through his and follows, playing as though she is with him. Paul smiles kindly as the two approach him, giving a slight nod of acknowledgment to his coworker.

"Can I help the two of you?" Paul inquires skeptically as he urges them to keep up with the group.

"I need to use the restroom," Sam explains softly so as not to be overheard by the other three guests. Gabbers nods in agreement while holding up two fingers.

"You both need to use the restroom? At the same time?" Paul quarries with mild amusement.

"We have been holding it awhile. We didn't really want to say anything, but we need to go pretty bad now." Sam explains softly once again.

"Well, we are getting ready to stop for an extended break on the third floor." Paul offers with a beaming smile. "We have a meal set up for you and the other guests along with some games and prizes." He adds with his hand on the small of their backs in an effort to keep them gathered with the rest of the group.

"If I might make an observation," Gabber remarks softly while looking at the backs of the other guests. "We seem to be short two guests. Are we not?" She remarks pointedly.

"We are," Paul admits disappointedly. "Two young women became frightened and wished to end their tour early. David and I led them out of the asylum earlier before returning." He offers an explanation much to the concern of Sam. Sam looks at Gabber

with wide eyes and an expression of fear
for his sister.

9.
Tuesday 02:49
(2:49 am)

Suzanne paces the stone floor of the padded room with her hands folded behind her back underneath her backpack. Angela sits in the corner with her knees drawn and hugged to her chest. The air in the room is becoming humid with their combined body heat and Suzanne's fuming frustration. She has not been able to get through to Sam in the immeasurable time they have spent in the padded chamber. Her one hope is that their captors will come back for them, allowing Suzanne to rush the door to attempt an escape. Her mind keeps toying with ideas on how she may trip the lock, but each one coming is as improbable as the last. She is about to take a seat next to Angela when she hears footsteps coming from outside in the corridor.

"Hurry, get over here." Suzanne urges Angela as she stands against the wall just to the left of the door. Angela rushes to join her as a shadow passes by the window of the door. Suzanne lowers her stance in preparations to tackle her way from the room, giving Angela a telling nod to run as soon as she has the assailant to the ground.

There is a brief moment of shuffling, an inaudible whispering before Suzanne and Angela can hear the recognizable screeching of the lever being lifted to the open position outside of the door. With an echoing clicking sound and the whirling of green light, the door pops open nearly half a foot with the swirling green light flooding out through the sliver of a crack. The two girls watch as a towering, boding shadow slivers through the growing opening of the doorway. Suzanne lowers herself slightly more while holding her arms firmly to her side. She has played tackle football with the boys and the one thing she learned, win or lose, the only way to earn their respect is by being able to take and give a proper hit. She has indeed broken a fair amount of bones. Both hers, and that of a headstrong boy who thought it wise to taunt her for being a girl.

At the first sign of a hard body, Suzanne rushes forth. She plunges her shoulder into the stomach of a fit male while wrapping her arms around his waist. She picks him up off of the floor before plunging forward to pin him to the floor. She calls out to Angela in a frantic urgency. Angela runs from the room back the way they initially came while Suzanne hops and thrusts her body from side to side in a struggle to keep the man, who is well fitted with great strength, pinned to the floor. She watches disdainfully as she watches Angela look back and come to a stop with an expression of surprise.

"Why ain't you running, Angela?" Suzanne calls while struggling to keep her target down.

"Because there is nothing to run from!" Suzanne hears Sam call from beneath her. " This is some great way to thank someone for freeing you." Suzanne releases him, sitting back on her heels to look at her brother with her hair gone wild, her clothes rustled, and her backpack askew on her back. She brushes locks of blonde hair from in front of her eyes to look at him with curiosity.

"What...How did you know we were down here?" Suzanne inquires in a low voice. "I tried calling for you on the radio and got nothing back but static. We have no idea who trapped us in there."

"I think the one named Paul did it," Sam grumbles as Gabbers helps him sit up from the cold dusty floor. "I overheard them talking about trapping two girls down here. We had to find the right moment to sneak away to come to look. The door to the basement was locked. I had to bust the knob and locking mechanisms to get through." He struggles to his feet while holding his gut. Suzanne gently climbs to her feet as well while dusting her hands off.

"They shut the tour down early," Sam informs them while using his right thumb to point towards the stairs leading to the floor above. "Something about liability since two of the guests continue to sneak off and go missing. They are out front waiting for the law to arrive for a search party so if you know a means of avoiding them, that would be great."

"There is a maintenance shaft down the hall. We can take it to the first-floor office, then the exit to the caretakers shed out back." Suzanne suggests in a surreal tone of exasperstion.

"Lead the way," Sam remarks impatiently with an arm still holding his stomach. Suzanne nods and leads Sam along with their two new friends to the maintenance shaft back to the first floor where she had noticed a hidden exit that she discerns leads to the caretaker's shed by way of a stone hall she can see from the side window. The shed holds shovels, rakes, and other means of keeping the grounds with an unlocked door standing barely cracked open. Looking out into the grounds, They can see the parking lot with only three vehicles waiting unattended. Suzanne can see no signs of the three tour attendants nor any form of law enforcement.

"I have the funny feeling the police are never coming," Suzanne remarks pointedly as she leads the way from the shed towards the parking lot across the front lawn.

Suzanne drags her feet as she takes hesitant strides across the lawn to the paved parking lot. Her fifty's sedan sits waiting just where she had parked it along with a yellow late model Volkswagen Bug and a station wagon dressed like a hearse. Suzanne chuckles, instantly relating the vehicles to the women who own them. She heads straight for her car, unlocking the doors and setting her backpack in the back seat.

"Gabbers offered to give me a lift home." Sam stammers while running his hand over his eyes. "Can I catch up with you in the morning?"

"Yeah." Suzanne yawns while opening her driver's door. "I'll call you and let you know when to meet me at the Malt Shop."

"Can I join as well?" Angela inquires with a broad smile. "I would like to see this through now that I have gotten to spend some time with you."

"Sure, here is my number," Suzanne replies. She pulls a card from her wallet in her back pocket and hands it to her. Suzanne had taken to carrying around business cards since starting her private eye business.

*******

The lonesome drive home goes quietly and uneventfully giving Suzanne plenty of time to think over the evening's endeavors. She can not help but return time and time to the conversation she had overheard between Paul and David. Their shady behavior and the disturbing conversation she had listened in on gives her little doubt they have something to do with this demand from the late Mr. Tuttle. Dustin, Dustin must be in on it as well. Possibly the ring leader, maybe. She scratches her fingers through her disheveled hair in frustration as she runs a red light, narrowly avoiding t-boning an S-10.

The driver blares their horn as it passes through the intersection, leaving Suzanne sitting in an awkward position blocking two lanes of traffic heading west on Jefferson. Suzanne inhales deeply before exhaling and shifting into reverse to restart the stalled engine of her sedan. She is about to pull the rest of the way through the intersection when a set of blue swirling lights come up behind her with a brief call from their siren. Grumbling, Suzanne uses her signal to let the cruiser know she is going to pull into the parking lot of a Super America service station before pulling from the middle of the street. She circles the well-lit parking lot before pulling into an angling spot in front of the swinging double doors advertising a forty-four-ounce slushy with a white dog holding the drink with two paws.

The cruiser pulls behind her car as she turns the engine off. Suzanne begins retrieving the necessary documents from the visor when she notices the form of a rather jolly appearing deputy stepping alongside her driver's door. The officer taps her window with the head of his flashlight, prompting her to roll it down. Suzanne gruffs, rather discouraged by the events leading up to this minute, but a smile quickly spreads across her face when she sees the friendly face of Darrel Black, a friend she had made in Mason County, West Virginia. He had aided them on a case involving a supposedly haunted manor while becoming friendly with her best friend Abby. Once the case was over, he followed them to Darlington County, Ohio, and became a deputy under Sam.

"Sort of late, even for you, Suzanne," Darrel comments while shining his flashlight into the dark interior of the late model Chevy sedan. "Everything okay?" He inquires cheerfully.

"Yea." Suzanne chuckles despite the tension she is holding back. "I took on a new case and I am on my way home, well....to Dean's. I got distracted in thought and ran the light. I'm sorry, Darrel." Suzanne remarks awkwardly while holding up her hands with her documentation.

"What kind of case are you on now?" Darrel asks curiously while gathering the papers from her.

"A woman being haunted by her late husband that died, supposedly died, in the asylum years ago," Suzanne replies with a sinking gut. "How is Abby?" She hasn't seen her friend since her house burnt down and all of her attention became self-involved. They have not talked in nearly a year. Suzanne knew she and Darrel had gotten married, she had been invited but chose not to go even though she was a bridesmaid. She had sunken into her own hole.

"She is good. About five months along now. She and the babies are healthy and doing well." Darrel replies calmly. He is busy reading her documents, not really paying her any mind.

"I didn't know the two of you were expecting, that is awesome." Suzanne remarks in enthusiastic awkwardness. "Tell Abby I miss her and that I am happy for you both." She insists with an earnest plea of misery.

"I will. Most certainly." Darrel replies. He looks away from her documents long enough to smile down at her in the car. "I am going to go to my cruiser for a moment to check a few things, I will be right back." He advises her before walking off. Darrel leaves her with crushing hopes and a knot growing to the size of a watermelon in her stomach.

Suzanne sits waiting patiently in the driver's seat of her sedan while watching Darrel step into his cruiser from her rearview mirror. Leaning back in the seat, she takes notice of her lack of attention to her friendship with Abby. Taking the moment to use the still quiet. She pulls her cell phone from her back pocket and opens the text app. Typing in Abby's name, she takes in a deep breath before typing a message.

*"Hello, Abby. I am so sorry I have not texted you sooner or called. Darrel just told me the good news. Bad way of finding out, I think I am about to get a ticket, or worse. I miss you dearly and hope to hear from you again. I am sincerely sorry for my absence. I promise to do better."* She types with a tear running down her cheek. She wipes it away and presses send.

Suzanne lays her phone on the seat beside her for several minutes while watching Darrel in her mirror. She watches as he takes a phone call, sitting back in his seat and looking forward. Her phone dings audibly, allowing the display ribbon to notify her of a message response from Abby. Suzanne picks her phone up to read the message with Abby inviting her to a baby shower this coming Saturday at their place. Abby advises her to be there at noon and that she is using the Pooh theme. Suzanne smiles broadly as she types a reply.

"*I wouldn't miss it.*" She replies grinning broadly. "*Need anything specific?*"

"*I have been searching everywhere for a circular baby crib. Can you find one?*" Abby replies with a grim emoji.

"*I will look,*" Suzanne replies with a blushing smiley face emoji.

Suzanne leans back, hearing Darrel closing his cruiser door and begin approaching her sedan. She sits her phone on the seat next to her once more and waits for him to approach. Darrel steps up beside the driver's door with his ticket book and her information in his hands. Suzanne smiles up at him, waiting for the worse.

"I am going to let you go on the reckless endangerment with the other vehicle, as well as the speeding and failure to use your signals. I do have to write you up for running the traffic light though since it was caught on the traffic light camera." Darrel advises her while ripping the ticket free of his book and hands it back to her with her information. "It is the least charge I can give you without either of us getting into serious trouble."

"I appreciate the courtesy." Suzanne remarks. She accepts the ticket along with her personal information.

"Thank you for texting her," Darrel comments while still standing next to her driver's door. "She has been extremely depressed the past few months. Hearing from you really lifted her spirits." Suzanne turns to look up at him with an awkward stutter.

"Made me feel better too," Suzanne replies casually.

"Don't let it be so long before you talk to her again. She has really missed you." Darrel instructs in a soft yet firm tone. "And I am able to pull you over anytime I please, Suzanne." Darrel threatens with a broad smile.

"I will keep that in mind." Suzanne remarks with a continued stammer. She smiles as if taking his statement as a joke, but the glare in his eyes tells her otherwise. She nods slowly and waits for him to reach his cruiser before starting her engine again.

Suzanne wastes no time once the swirling blue lights of Darrel's cruiser cease. Shifting into gear, she pulls back out onto the roadway with a direct twenty to thirty-minute drive remaining before she reaches Dean's house.

******

Pulling into the waiting garage door, Suzanne allows the car to coast to a stop with the engine off. It is nearly dawn when she closes the garage door and uses the side door to enter the house itself. She heads straight to her room, creeping quietly so as not to wake Aunt Francis or disturb Dean. She manages to reach the second floor without making a sound before the door to Dean's room opens as he steps out dressed for the day's work. He turns to see her standing in the hall and smiles broadly. His sleek black hair is swept to the right, his gray mechanic coveralls opened at the top to reveal a white tee shirt. He carries a duffle bag on his shoulder with fresh clothing to change into before coming home.

"I didn't expect you until this evening." Dean remarks with a glowing smile.

"The tour ended early," Suzanne replies with a bashful smile. She nibbles on her lower lip as he approaches her. His arms wrap around her, allowing Suzanne to lay her head on his shoulder and wrap her arms around his chest. Her backpack shifts on her back as he engulfs her in a deep hug, his breath brushing her ear as the hair around it flutters. She leans back slightly and leans inwards to give him a much-desired kiss before pulling away and looking into his eyes again.

"The offer still stands, anytime you want to consider it," Dean whispers with a handsome smile.

"There is a lot to consider, Dean." Suzanne stammers as she lowers her gaze.

"When won't there be, honestly, Suzanne." Dean remarks as he crouches to get within her gaze again.

"You have a point, but what about the living situation? I do not want to leave the farm. I will be going back as soon as it is ready." Suzanne points out as she motions around the lush house he owns. "It will not be as nice as this, even when brand new, but I want to be there."

"I will live there with you," Dean replies earnestly. "Anywhere, so long as I am with you."

"Dean, you don't really want to marry me. I get into trouble too much. I am trouble. I bring trouble and danger with every case I work." Suzanne urges him with a grimace. "I can't ask you to step into that."

"How often have I already? Always of my own choice. I will join you in any adventure you take on, no matter how dangerous." Dean replies with sincere energy and devotion. "There are no excuses left, Suzanne. I know what I would be getting into and I am still fully engaged in spending the rest of my life with you. Anytime you are willing." He slides his hands down to take hers while crouching to one knee. Holding out a small chiseled oak box, he opens it with his thumb to reveal an emerald gem on a solid gold band. Suzanne raises her free left hand to cover her mouth as tears trail down her eyes.

"I know this is like my third time proposing, and you have already made it clear you want to wait. I have waited for you my entire life, Suzanne, and I want to know right now while in this moment, will you marry me?" Dean proposes in a low whisper. Suzanne just looks at him with a mixture of admiration and overwhelming joy. They had been engaged once, for a short time, but had ended it because she was not ready. Not ready.  A sentiment she has clung to for nearly a year, putting her true fears and feelings on the back burner. Now, with him kneeling before her and every excuse exhausted, she decides it is time to face her fears and follow her heart.

"Dean," She whispers as she offers her left hand. "Yes, yes I will." She replies with tear-filled eyes and a broad smile. Dean places the ring on her finger before rising to embrace her in a deep, loving hug. They share a gentle yet endearing kiss before releasing.

"I can call off work so we can celebrate." Dean offers with a giddy, stammering voice.

"No, go to work first." Suzanne replies as she fiddles with the new ring while lying against his chest. "I had a long night, so I will most likely be sleeping all day and you have two projects in your garage. We can celebrate this evening."

"I will invite everyone over for a cookout," Dean suggests while embracing her snugly in his arms.

"That will be great," Suzanne replies, looking up at him. She kisses him again before lying her head against his chest and closing her eyes. "I'm going to shower and crawl into your bed to sleep."

They hold one another for several more minutes before Suzanne walks him to the garage door and sees him off. Once the house is locked up once more, she returns to her room to get a change of clothes and set her bookbag on her bed. Retrieving a towel and washcloth from the pantry, she showers quickly before sitting under the rain head of the shower, basking in the warm water while collecting her thoughts. It has been a long night with many revelations. It was certainly interesting, all of the scandals leading up to Darrel pulling her over, her reuniting text with Abby, and the final proposal of Dean. She has much to think about.

Turning the water off, she dries and dresses in her boy shorts and tank top before disposing of the dirty laundry in the hamper. She wraps her long, wet blonde hair in a towel before making her way back to her room for her phone and backpack. Smiling with a beaming smile, she nibbles her lower lip before making her way to Dean's room down the hall. Turning the lush black silk sheets and fur-lined silk blanket, she crawls into the bed and plugs her phone in. She barely rolls to her side and covers before she finds herself in a deep sleep, her hair still bound in the towel.

10.<br>
Tuesday 12:11 pm

Suzanne wakes to the screaming of Aunt Francis somewhere outside of Dean's room. Tossing the sheets and blanket aside, she rushes from Dean's room into the hall. Stumbling into the wall with her right shoulder, Suzanne rushes to the stairs leading to the first floor where Aunt Francis' room rests. She can hear a struggle and muffled screaming coming from the sitting room as she takes the stairs three at a time.

Suzanne enters the sitting room to see a masked man in a black long sleeve shirt and blue jeans. The sofa that had been turned with its back towards the stairs is now overturned with the cushions flung about the room. The lamp and end table are broken with shards of the light bulb scattered towards the door. The masked figure has his back to the stairs where Suzanne has just reached the first floor. Aunt Francis is struggling against his powerful arms, a gag tied around her mouth and both of her hands behind her back. What little fight she is able to give runs out as she notices Suzanne.

The masked man turns just in time to see Suzanne rush from the stairs, using the overturned sofa as a stepping stool as she lunges through the air open-armed. Aunt Francis manages to break free as his attention diverts to Suzanne. With her out of the way, Suzanne fully lands her left shoulder into his sternum and raps her arms around him as she takes him to the floor in a great thud. Rising to her knees, Suzanne catches the man trying to sit up with a right hook to his temple. The man immediately checks out, falling unconscious to the floor where his head lobs from side to side before becoming still.

Suzanne climbs to her feet, bruising already forming on her shoulder and knees as she makes her way over to her terrified Aunt. Removing the gag and bindings on her Aunt's wrists, Suzanne's gaze comes across an ominous plain black van parked outside along the curb. The window in the corner of the sitting room is shattered, a chilly wind causing the curtains to flutter in the room. Suzanne crouches next to the window in an effort to note the license plate number but finds it blacked out with dark paper. There are no signs or identifying remarks of any kind on the exterior of the van that she can notice in her frantic state. Determined to get some kind of information that relates to the intruders, Suzanne rushes past the horrified Aunt Francis, out of the front door in her tank top and boy shorts, and barefooted.

Suzanne leaps from the porch in mid-stride towards the mysteriously unmarked van, running at full speed with those in the neighborhood or in the streets looking at her with expressions of disgust and curiosity. Two figures are barely visible in the front seats of the van. One is a larger male with a beard, the other seems to be a leaner, more meek figure. The leaner figure nudges the larger hastily when he notices Suzanne running towards them. As she crosses the front yard, the van motor turns over and starts with a loud bang. Suzanne instinctively tries to skid to a stop, causing her feet to slide out in front of her as she falls to her bottom with her hands outstretched behind her. The van pulls off loudly with a trail of black smoke left in its wake.

Suzanne watches the van speed away without so much as one of the other citizens asking a question. She gets the feeling those in this neighborhood are familiar with the shady activity and the 'No Questions Asked' routine of survival. She slowly climbs to her feet while watching to see what direction the van takes at the intersection before remembering her aunt is currently in the house with an unconscious kidnapper. Abandoning the surveillance on the van, she rushes back inside just in time to catch Aunt Francis standing over the unconscious man with a cast iron egg skillet held clumsily aloft in her arms. Not wanting her to get hurt, Suzanne runs over to her and takes the skillet into her own hands.

"Dean keeps zip ties in the drawer under the microwave," Suzanne remarks with a smile. "Will you fetch them for me?" Suzanne suggests while twirling the skillet over to a recliner in the corner. Aunt Francis grumbles as she leaves the sitting room returning a short time later with long, thick black zip ties.

Before removing the man's mask, she binds his wrists together with one zip tie on each wrist intertwined. She then removes his boots and socks before doing likewise with his ankles. She makes for certain they are snug enough to faintly cut into the flesh. After she is certain he is restrained, she empties his pockets while searching for any form of weapon. All she finds is a Buck knife hidden in his right hip pocket. No wallet, no identification. Looking at his mask curiously, she crouches by his head and removes the ski mask to find David from the asylum tour hidden within.

Sitting with her back to the fireplace behind her, she hugs her knees while thinking back on the conversation she had overheard during the tour the night before. Concern, not only for her safety but also for Aunt Francis' becomes suddenly real. Her past experiences with danger and her loved ones being taken revive themselves in her mind as flashbacks to such times plague her vision. The smell of her house burning down as she ascends the driveway to find it in embers wafts into her senses with the breeze from the broken window.

She did this. She may not have directly bound and gagged her precious Aunt, but she welcomed it to happen by accepting the case. By agreeing to work the case, she invited terrible monsters into not her home this time but Dean's and for unsafe conditions to threaten her loved ones again. Climbing to her feet, she rushes upstairs to grab her backpack with Aunt Francis calling after her. Not hesitating for a moment, she rushes back downstairs where she cups Aunt Francis' arm with her own and leads her out to the garage where she uses her car keys to unlock the car doors.

"What in the blue blazes is going on?" Aunt Francis inquires in a high-pitched voice as Suzanne urges her into the passenger seat.

"We are going to Sam's," Suzanne replies before closing the passenger door. As she walks around the car, she presses the open button by the rolling garage door and approaches the driver's door. Climbing in, she sets her backpack in the middle of the bench seat and dials Sam's number. Sam answers just as she pulls out onto the street.

"Aunt Francis and I are on our way to your house, now!" Suzanne remarks pointedly.

"I'm not home," Sam replies with an exhausted tone of concern. "What is going on?"

"They tried to take her." Suzanne remarks as an angry tear rolls down her left cheek. "They tried, and they tried again. They tried to take her while I was sleeping and I just barely got to her in time."

"Who tried to take who, Suzanne?" Sam asks with renewed vigor. "What is going on? You're not making any sense."

"The man from the asylum came. He tried to take her." Suzanne replies. Aunt Francis shakes her shoulder from the passenger seat. Suzanne holds the shifter in her right hand, the car still setting in the middle of the street with traffic frozen in both lanes. Horns begin to blare from frustrated motorists as she continues to talk to Sam on the phone.

"They broke into Dean's home and tried to take her, Sam. All because I took this case." Suzanne whimpers. "Every time I take a case, every time, the people I love get hurt or taken and they have already started this time." She calls into the phone.

"Where are you, sis? I will come to you." Sam remarks with a series of heavy breathing on the other end of the call.

"I'm in front of Dean's," Suzanne replies as she releases her hold on the clutch. The car hops forward into the front bumper of an Orange Nissan jarring the car and the driver inside. A woman climbs from the car as Suzanne's sedan stalls out and dies, yelling frantically. Aunt Francis climbs from the passenger seat to apologize to the woman and explain the situation. In the distance, Suzanne can just make out the wailing of police sirens.

"Did you notify the police?" Suzanne inquires as tears begin to stream in a steady flow down her cheeks.

"Yeah...." Sam replies slowly. There is a moment of silence before he returns. "Wait there. I am on my way." Sam assures her before hanging up the call. Suzanne drops her phone into the floorboard and wraps herself in a hug before she begins crying. She turns sideways in the seat and draws her knees to her chest with her feet in the seat. The sounds of horns blowing from either direction do nothing to sate her agony and guilt. Quivering and crying, she burrows her chin into her chest and lays against the seat. She does not notice Aunt Francis calling Dean.

## 11.
### Tuesday 13:25
### (1:25 pm)

Sam arrives on the scene at Dean's house to find Suzanne having a mental breakdown in the seat of her sedan. Aunt Francis is talking to an officer, retelling the events of the morning. An officer is attempting to speak with Suzanne through the open window to no avail. Dean is pulling up to the blockade that the police have set up three blocks on either end of the street, blocking off any intersecting streets. Several blocks of traffic have accumulated with angry motorists being directed by police officers. Darrel approaches Sam, carrying a sheriff's shield and his sidearm.

"I was hoping to see you when the call came through," Darrel remarks with a smile as he hands Sam his badge and revolver. "I grabbed these from your desk so you could take over lead authority on the scene."

"Thanks, Darrel," Sam replies as he reluctantly clips the badge onto his belt on his left hip and his revolver with the holster on his right hip. "Have you discovered anything compelling?" Sam inquires curiously with a tone of concern as he waves for the junior officers to allow Dean entrance.

"Your sister is not talking. We can't get anything from her." Darrel remarks as he puffs out his stomach and exhales audibly. "She hasn't stopped crying long enough to say anything. Your aunt, on the other hand, is a tough old bird."

"Tell me something I don't know." Sam groans. "What has she said?"

"A man in a ski mask startled her in the kitchen. She fought back or tried to at least. He gagged and bound her after a struggle. That's when she saw Suzanne coming down the stairs. The man didn't notice her coming until it was too late. She leaped across the overturned sofa and tackled him to the ground, punched him and knocked him out, then ran out of the house to try and catch the van." Darrel takes a deep breath before continuing to catch Sam up on the situation. "When she couldn't stop the van, she went back into the house and bound the man's wrists and ankles with thick zip ties. When she removed the mask, Aunt Francis got the impression Suzanne recognized him. That's when Suzanne tried to leave the house with her and....now we are here."

"Let me talk to her," Sam instructs as he and Darrel approach the sedan. The junior officer trying with no result to speak with Suzanne nods and steps away. Sam looks at him and Darrel pointedly until they accept the hint and move on to give him some space.

"Suzanne," Sam speaks soothingly. "Scoot over and let me in too." He instructs carefully. Suzanne, sitting quivering with her feet in the seat and her knees hugged to her chest slowly begins to scoot across the seat with her back still to Sam and the driver's door. Sam opens the door and climbs in under the steering wheel before closing the door again.

"Sheriff," a senior officer on the scene calls out to him. "Can you move the car from the middle of the road so we can move traffic through?"

Sam gives him a nod before starting the engine. Once he is in the driveway, parking just in front of the open garage door, he kills the engine. Wrapping an arm around Suzanne's shoulders and chest, he draws her into him comfortingly and kisses the back of her head. Suzanne turns around and leans into him with her face hidden in his chest.

"Suzanne," He sighs deeply and closes his eyes. Seeing her in this state has him deeply concerned as he has only ever seen her stronger unwavering side. "I need you to pull it together and fill me in on what has you so bothered." She quivers for several minutes, the tears thankfully rapidly drying up. Suzanne pulls a handkerchief from her glovebox and blows her nose before looking at him with tear-streaked cheeks, red swollen eyes, and a red face.

"There was a moment in the asylum when I was hidden in the vent. I could hear David and Paul, the tour guides, talking about me. It didn't bother me so much then because I am used to pointless threats. You know, the ones that come across as all bark and no bite." Suzanne blows her nose again as Aunt Francis climbs into the passenger seat pinning Suzanne in the middle. "It was David that attacked Aunt Francis. The man I caught in the house. I have no doubt the two men in the van were Paul and Dustin." She informs Sam with earnest conviction. "When I overheard them, they had recognized me and that I was there investigating. They knew I was learning and finding clues. They spoke of methods or means of dealing with me in the basement. It was one of them that locked us in the room."

"They locked the two of you in there then canceled the rest of the tour." Sam remarks nodding. "They were going to make it look like the two of you left or disappeared, that made them cancel the tour. They faked leaving until all the guests were gone then they would come back and deal with the two of you." Sam finishes her thought while leaning back into the seat.

"They were willing to kill me, make me disappear, and let the legend of the asylum take the credit," Suzanne confirms his theory before blowing her nose again.

"Things like that have never bothered you before," Sam observes the change in attitude and presses slightly. "You have had more than your fair share of close calls and it has never shaken you like this."

Suzanne lowers her gaze as she draws her feet onto the edge of the seat and hugs her knees. She is no longer crying but sniffling with a runny nose. Aunt Francis scoots closer, urging Suzanne to say what is on her mind, tell them what has her so afraid or shaken. Suzanne hesitates for several minutes before speaking.

"I never considered the consequences of my cases to my life let alone that of my loved ones," Suzanne admits sheepishly. "At least, not thoroughly. The thought crossed my mind, but I always figured I was able to keep everyone safe. I thought I was still in control." She takes in a deep breath before continuing to rock back and forth in the seat while hugging her legs. Her bare legs in her boy shorts and her bare arms reveal goosebumps with very fine streaks of veins in the undersides of her arms.

"It has dawned on me that Aunt Francis has been kidnapped several times now, with another attempt this morning." Suzanne exhales with a quivering voice. Her lower lip quivers with a threat of fresh tears swelling in her eyes. "Our home was burned down because of me. Loved ones have been hurt or taken, and others have been hurt. I lost my job at the law firm with Brandon. And now, with Dean and I actually and properly engaged with the aspect of really getting married this time, there is even more risk with even more to lose." Suzanne stammers as she begins to cry again. "All I do is bring danger, terror, and destruction to our family. I have brought nothing but disaster since I have started."

"I have known you to lie before, Suzanne." Aunt Francis remarks after several moments of thoughtful silence within the car. "I have been ashamed and embarrassed by you since I started looking after your brother and yourself. I have never stopped loving you, keep mindful, but I have had my regrets." She hesitates a moment as she uses her apron to wipe away her own tears. "But I have never been prouder of you than I have these past several years as I watched you aspire and grow as a private detective." She remarks sternly. "I know there have been dangerous moments, but you and your brother have always kept us safe. The house may have been destroyed, but you are having it rebuilt as it was, only stronger. Things lost can be replaced, truly."

"Suzanne, you have become a sense of pride in the family," Sam admits awkwardly. "I have, and so has Aunt Francis, we have bragged to literally everyone on you. I have been kinda hung up on things going on in my own life, we all have, but we are with you always. You are one of the strongest women I know. Aside from Aunt Francis, of course."

"I know there will always be a danger, sweety," Aunt Francis uses her wrinkled, vein covered cold hand to raise Suzanne's chin so Suzanne is looking into her eyes. "Nothing good in life comes without risks or challenges. You have helped so many in Darlington County, and other areas. You and your brother, him as the sheriff and you as the private detective, the two of you are my greatest source of pride in life. The two of you have become steeples in the community. You need to remain steadfast with your convictions, follow your guts, and finish your case. You will keep us safe, I know you will. So, stop worrying."

Suzanne turns to look at her Aunt, her red puffy blue eyes stinging as she strains her vision through the tears. Her Aunt simply smiles at her with a warm, loving expression of love and comfort. Suzanne lunges forth, wrapping her arms around Aunt Francis, drawing her in close for a snug hug. Sam reaches over to pat her on the back in a brotherly, assuring way as he tosses his head to the side with a smirk.

"Besides, if you don't solve this mystery, there is a new private eye in town ready to take the case," Sam informs her with a chuckle, knowing this will get her full attention. Suzanne turns towards him briskly with furrowed eyebrows and clenched fists.

"Who?" She inquires in stern jealousy.

"Some guy by the name of Richard Parsons from Buffalo, West Virginia. He came into town early this morning after hearing about your alleged disappearance from the asylum." Sam replies coyly. "Darrel was telling me about him on the walk here from my car."

"Well, send him back. This is my case." Suzanne retorts stubbornly.

"That is my girl." Aunt Francis smirks and raises her fist swiftly. "That is the attitude. Now, go take it back."

12.
Tuesday 17:22
(5:22 pm)

The barn of her home looms ahead of the driveway in the early evening light. Its faded gray and splotchy spots of red or brown come as a welcoming sight to Suzanne as she pulls up the driveway of her home to find the construction crew just finishing up for the day. The foreman, a rather burly and almost attractive man of dark complexion, stands by the tool truck in his sleeveless white shirt soaked with sweat and a pair of dirty, dust-covered denim jeans. He is relieving the work hat from his smooth head, placing it in a storage compartment on the side of his truck bed when Suzanne pulls to a stop a few feet away. Twelve other men are placing tools in the storage compartments of the truck bed as she climbs out to the welcoming smile of the foreman.

Behind the work crew, the newly restored farmhouse Suzanne had presented the design for stands with the shell intact. A thick sheet of white protective laminate covers the outer wall waiting for siding to be applied. The name and logo of the local hardware store shimmer in blue in several places, a shadowing advert for anyone who can see the house from the adjacent road. It was all there, just as she remembers the original house, only newer and stronger than before. It will not have all of the familiar creaks, sounds, smells, or faded colors she had grown accustomed to, but instead, it would pave the way for new memories and a growing family.

"Ms. Sturgeon," The foreman addresses her in a deep booming voice. "What a pleasure to see you this evening. What do you think?" He inquires as he motions to the house behind him. "Only a few months off of the schedule."

"It looks perfect from the outside," Suzanne admits with a feeling of joy and overwhelming anxiousness swelling within. "How far along are you inside?" She asks as she turns her gaze towards him.

"We have the first floor framed, walls up and flooring down. The stairs are finished aside from a final sanding and clear coat." The foreman shrugs with his right shoulder and teeters tottering in the air. "The second floor and attic are framed and insulated. The floor is down in the hall and two of the rooms. The plumbing is in as well as the electric. Just waiting on the electric inspection to be completed. So far we have not hit any true issues aside from timing."

"Do you think we will be back in there before Christmas, Jake?" Suzanne asks hopefully. She holds her hand up to showcase the engagement ring with a beaming smile. "It would be great to spend this Christmas in my home."

"Congratulations, Ms. Sturgeon," Jake responds jovially while clapping his large, muscular hands together. His biceps and forceps flex with every movement, rippling and filled with raw strength. "I am sure we can get you home soon, possibly even before Thanksgiving." He boasts with a jolly, almost child-like tone. If not for his size and naturally alerting appearance, Suzanne would easily consider him a sensitive or soft-hearted person. As it is, you have to get past the exterior appearance in order to see these traits about the man.

******

Suzanne pulls in front of the Sheriff's office, parking alongside Sam's El Camino just a few cars down from the entrance. Shifting her sedan into gear, she shuts the engine off before climbing from her car with her backpack slung over her right shoulder. Her Muck Boots land in a puddle of water from the rain that had just ended. The skies are still filled with dark clouds, a cool cold breeze fleeing briskly through the air. Leaves fall from the trees that can be found along the sidewalks of every street. Suzanne takes in a deep breath while smiling broadly.

"I love the fall weather." She remarks under her breath. Smiling with a new and brighter sense of life, she enters the Sheriff's office in search of her brother. She approaches an elderly receptionist behind a high desk littered with papers, documents, and wanted posters picturing the deputies to be hung for Halloween. The elderly woman has curly white hair in a snood. Her white blouse is embroidered at the collar with rose petals. She slams a stamp on a document as Suzanne steps up to the counter that spans three-quarters of the entrance. The remaining section has a swinging gate that allows entry to the office itself. Chairs line the walls of the lobby with a few tables decorated with magazines.

"Is Sam in his office?" Suzanne inquires rather jovially.

"He is in an interrogation room." She responds as she looks up to smile at Suzanne. "He said you could wait in his office if you arrived before he finished." She waves Suzane through with a beaming smile. Suzanne nods to her before going to the swinging door and passes through with several of the officers sitting at their desks looking up at her and waving.

Suzanne makes her way to the hall where she finds the door to Sam's office as the first door on the left with the door diagonally opposite opens to the break room. The smell of a fresh pot of coffee wafts through the open door.

Opening the door to his office, Suzanne enters the dimly lit, atmospheric room to find the window curtains drawn closed. A salt rock fills the room with changing tones of light while a tart burner in the opposite corner gives off a lavender scent. Sam's desk and swivel chair is positioned in front of the window, the walls lined with bookshelves displaying all manner of law books and anime graphic crime novels. Two chairs rest opposite the desk from Sam's swivel chair. A desktop computer screen sets at an angle on the desk with a keyboard close by, and several trays of documents rest in the opposite corner.

Suzanne sits in one of the chairs, placing her backpack in the other. Opening her bag, she pulls out her ledger and voice recorder. She had transferred the recordings to her laptop the previous night so the device is emptily readied to be filled. Crossing her right leg over her left in her denim jeans, she begins making notes of the day thus far and her conversation with Jake. She waits only a short twenty minutes before Sam enters the room in a button-down green shirt and dark blue denim jeans over black leather blues. Cracking his knuckles, he sits at his desk and leans back before exhaling.

"Did you learn anything from our intruder?" Suzanne inquires, breaking right to the point of her visit.

"No," Sam replies disappointedly. "He insists he was acting alone and that the van you saw was not related to his crime." He informs her with a tone of discouragement. "He refuses to admit his co-workers were in on it and denies any actions that were taken or insinuated against you at the asylum. He refuses to ever speak of doing you any harm or knowing that you would be at the house he just happened to choose at random to break into and rob."

"Has he lawyered up?" Suzanne asks with a stern tone.

"He didn't have to," Sam replies while holding something back. "One was hired for him by a second party."

"Just out of generosity?" Suzanne remarks skeptically. "Who is his council? I will have them know who they are protecting." She remarks with her gaze at her ledger where she makes notes.

"Brandon Bailes," Sam replies quickly. Suzanne raises her gaze to reveal the wide-eyed appearance of disbelief. "They hired Brandon to represent him."

"Why do the worst of people always hire the best attorney in town that just happens to be my boss? Well, ex-boss and friend." Suzanne remarks sourly as she sits back in the chair. She pulls her cell phone from her back pocket and texts Brandon quickly.

*"We need to meet about your recent defendant, Paul."* She messages him quickly. *"He is the subject of one of my cases and attempted to nab Aunt Francis."* She lays her phone on her knee and returns her gaze to Sam.

"Did he give anything? Even the slightest nibble?" Suzanne presses pointedly as she uncrosses her legs only to cross the left leg over the right. Her left boot toe sways to the song she had heard on the car radio on her way in.

"Nothing. We couldn't even get him to react to facts we already know." Sam replies with a yawn of exhaustion.

"Did you make it home okay after we visited the asylum?" Suzanne inquires curiously as she begins putting her things away. Her phone vibrates with a new message she fully intends on opening once she has her things stowed away safely.

"Hmmm?" Sam replies before quickly adding to his response. "Yeah, yeah. Sure did." He adds awkwardly. "She dropped me off at home, waited until I was in the door, and pulled away. I did take her phone number though. Just in case there is cause to contact her with further questions or requests."

"Yeah, I took Angela's number as well." Suzanne remarks as she sits back in her seat. Her full attention is on the message Brandon had sent, her focus too occupied to hear the subtle difference in Sam's responses or awkward tone. "Brandon just replied to my text. He wants me to book an appointment with his receptionist tomorrow. I've never had to book an appointment with him."

"You don't work for him anymore." Sam points out with a sigh of relief though his concern for further questioning of his time with Gabbers does not fully dissipate. "With the relationship the two of you shared, It is not hard to believe he wants it to be more professional now rather than two friends when it comes to cases."

"That will not settle well," Suzanne mutters. She begins typing once more. "This has to be resolved so I can just go when I need to rather than wait. Plus, I need access, full access without question, to his files."

"I don't think you are going to get that again," Sam remarks reluctantly. All the while Suzanne is texting Brandon.

*"Also, I would like to ask about getting my job back now that the probationary period is over?"* She sends the message with a brief pause before adding another line of query. *"I was hoping we could meet this evening and talk about it, like professional equals, but still a friendly atmosphere."* She adds with a smirk. *"I miss my job there, my position at your law firm. I think I am or can still be an asset."*

"Are you going to try and question him before I send him to a cell to await arraignment?" Sam asks hurriedly. "I need to arrange it if so before I leave for the evening."

"What, do you have a hot date or something?" Suzanne remarks sarcastically with a chuckle.

"Not exactly," Sam replies with blushing cheeks. "A support meeting for men whose wives have left them. A divorced man help group." He explains. Suzanne looks up from her phone to examine him.

"Oh," She responds with an awkward expression. "In that case, yeah. Arrange it and go on with your evening." Suzanne adds with her cheeks beginning to blush in the embarrassment of her insulting remark to her brother. A text comes through as she sits shifting in her seat trying to think of something supportive to say on the subject. She grunts, clears her throat and opens the message to read it.

"*I can meet you at the Malt Shop around nine tonight, but only as friends.*" Brandon's message does not lean on the optimistic air of conversations. "*No promises.*"

*"I understand, but I am sincerely sorry for the trouble I caused and would very much like my position back."* She replies with several emojis.

*"What about your private practice?"* Brandon responds after several minutes.

*"I want to do both, I can do both. It will help get my house finished soon too with the added income."* She adds with a boost of energy in the hope of getting her job back.

"I have an appointment with Brandon at the Malt Shop around nine this evening." Suzanne relays her conversation to Sam who continues to sit awkwardly in his swivel chair behind his desk. "Do you want to join me?"

"I don't think so," Sam replies. He begins to breathe a little easier with the conclusion that she had either dropped or not noticed the awkwardness of the Gabbers conversation. "I will be resting at home at that time."

"Good point. I think Dean will just be getting home from the hardware store with a new window." Suzanne remarks sourly. "I tried to give him the money to replace it, but he refused to take it. Insists on covering the price himself. Must be a man thing. He won't let me pay for anything while we have been staying there. Now that we are engaged, it is even worse. I can't complain though, he is good to us." She rambles on for several minutes as she finishes putting her things away. "I think I might be able to get my job back with him, one last time, and have an extra income coming in."

"Well, wait here," Sam remarks as he stands up and makes his way around his desk. "I will go make arrangements for you to sit with Paul before I go. They will come in to get you here." He pats her on the shoulder before exiting his office and calling for Deputy Darrel Black.

"See Suzanne to interrogation room three where the suspect is being held," Sam instructs casually. "She will wait in my office until you get her. Have One of the junior deputies sit with her until she is finished. Just as a precaution." He adds as his voice trails off on his way from the building.

It is a matter of minutes before Darrel comes in to see her to the interrogation rooms in the back of the building. The holding cells are in the basement. They rest down a set of stairs at the end of the hall where the rooms are accessed. Suzanne enters the interrogation room to see Paul sitting handcuffed to a stainless steel table opposite the entrance where a junior detective stands just inside of the door waiting on her. Suzanne sits down across the table from him with her voice recorder on and recording. She spends just under an hour questioning him. She tries a gentle, persuasive approach at first offering her help in exchange for his cooperation. When that doesn't work, she tries aggression. Neither approach is to any avail.

With her questioning gaining nothing of any use, she relinquishes the interrogation and leaves the police station. Climbing into her sleek black coupe, she quickly calls Angela instructing her to meet at the Malt Shop around nine. Suzanne gives her explicit instructions to sit at a separate table from her and observe the man she meets with. Smiling, Suzanne gives her a particular set of instructions as a train begins traveling the set of tracks only a few blocks away. The sound of the warning bells echoes over the call. Once her instructions are given, Suzanne gets off of the phone and starts the coupe's engine. Backing from her parking spot, she exits onto the road and heads towards the Malt Shop.

13.
Tuesday 20:49
(8:49 pm)

Suzanne sits at her customary table in the Malt Shop in the back corner facing the door. Her usual order has just been delivered. Two double Malt Burgers, a basket of fries with sweet and sour sauce, and a large strawberry milkshake are set in front of her as she rests her backpack in the seat next to her, the voice recorder ready to be activated. Angela sits at the table nearest hers with easy access to the chair where Suzanne aims for Brandon to occupy. She is dressed in her usual black leather with a halter top and mini skirt. It is ten to nine when Brandon finally enters the Malt shop in his customary business suit, briefcase, and trench coat. He places his order with instructions on where to deliver it before approaching the seat opposite Suzanne and taking his seat.

"I would be lying if I said I had not anticipated this meeting. Both for your position and the case you spoke of." Brandon remarks as he hangs his coat over the chair housing his briefcase just a few feet from him. "Tell me, where are you on the case?" Suzanne takes a sip of her milkshake and tilts her head downward briefly before clearing her throat and raising her gaze to meet his once more.

"I have a strong case against him," Suzanne remarks sternly. "I have voice recordings and photos from the asylum detailing the threat I gave the police." She eats a few fries and takes a bite from her burger while he sits in deep interest. Inhaling deeply, she exhales through her nose while chewing. Once she is content he is fully interested, she swallows her bite and wipes her mouth with her napkin. "What I want, I want some strong level of cooperation in exchange for my help in reducing his sentence." She shrugs with a broad smile, knowing she has him right where she needs him. "Oh, and my job back." She adds quickly.

Brandon sits back briefly, his gaze on her the entire time with no regard for anything that is going on around him. He examines her quickly but with wise eyes, knowing most of the signs to look for when determining her intent. Suzanne's smile broadens when he leans forward with his elbows on the table. He cups his hands together while resting his chin on them with beady eyes.

"Can you get the crime reduced to a minor offense with minimal jail time or even house arrest?" Brandon inquires in a low voice.

"I can manage three months with another nine months of house arrest." Suzanne counters sternly. "That is a good deal, I am sure. I checked based on his priors."

"In exchange for what?" Brandon asks curiously. "I am not sure what all you are seeking nor what all is available."

"I want the entire operation," Suzanne instructs plainly. "I want the names and locations of everyone trying to pull one over on Mrs. Tuttle. I want the entire plan, where to find the base of operations, and who the ring leader is. I want it all." Suzanne presses, leaving no doubt on how far she is willing to take this case. "And, my job back."

"About your job," Brandon stammers. He pulls his business suit, unbuttoning the coat and flapping it open. "Have you heard of Richard Parsons?" Brandon inquires with furrowed brows. Suzanne instantly begins to growl in rage.

"You know I am ten times the detective he is." She snaps rather loudly, causing many in the diner to turn and look at her. The distraction draws all attention squarely to her as the Malt Shop goes eerily silent for several long moments.

"Yes, I agree," Brandon replies hesitantly. "What I want, as I restore your position at the law firm, is your word that you will close this case before he does." Brandon offers in a voice just audible over the busy noise of the diner, the occupants all of which are now talking about Suzanne and their interaction.

"I can assure you, after hearing what information you can arrange for me from Paul, I will have a clear direction to my next action in the sequence that will place me closing the case," Suzanne promises him boldly. "I firmly believe he holds the keys to the case. If he is willing and honest. I need him to be open and truthful or the deal is off."

"I will run the offer by him, and encourage him to accept." Brandon assures her with a friendly smile. It is about this time his order arrives at the table. The young waitress in a pink blouse and mini skirt arrives, setting a tray down in front of him. He offers her a ten-dollar bill as a tip before she walks away. Thanking him, she takes the bill and disappears into the busy noise of the diner. Brandon eats several fries and takes a long sip of his vanilla milkshake. "Come into the building tomorrow and sign in with my new receptionist. Just so she knows you."

"Who do you have now?" Suzanne inquires casually as she swallows a wad of fries.

"Some girl straight out of high school. Her mom is a former alliance I had to make in the University." Brandon replies awkwardly. "She is a clumsy girl, but her intentions are well meant. She is entering her first year of law school and not sure if she is in the right field of study, so her mom thought it would be good for her to work at a known law firm in an entry-level position."

"I will come by tomorrow and you can give me my job back officially," Suzanne smirks with a mouth full of her burger.

"I will warn the staff on the first floor you are coming." Brandon jests as he wipes his hands with a napkin. He pokes fun at her for the dirty tricks she has played on the elderly attendant that guards the elevators to the upper floors. Suzanne has gone as far as to fill the foyer with smoke to sneak past the elderly man and gain access to the lifts.

"That may be a wise choice." Suzanne jokes back.

******

Suzanne and Angela pull into the gloom-filled parking lot of the old asylum where a group of nearly two dozen gather. Dustin and David stand near the front of the group in plain, noticeable reflective shirts. Each wears a portable hand radio on their hips and a distant, disgruntled expression. A new member of their trio, a dark-complected woman with wavy brown hair and denim jeans aside from her reflective shirt, is trying to herd the visitors into a manageable cluster as the tour is set to begin.

"Hello, all." the young woman calls out audibly for everyone to hear. "I am Jackie, and I would like to welcome you to the West Gate Asylum for the Criminally Insane." She gestures with her arms held out wide for a moment, likely expecting applause as far as Suzanne can figure. "It is nearly time for us to begin, so if you will just check in with me," She holds a clipboard in the air situated in her left hand. "I will take your tickets and we will begin once everyone has checked in." Suzanne smiles broadly as she pulls their tickets from her backpack and approaches Jackie with Angela by her side.

"Welcome, Mr. and Mrs. Edmonts. We are pleased to have you with us this evening." Jackie greets the elderly pair ahead of Suzanne.

Jackie's smile does not hesitate even briefly as Suzanne steps forward with their tickets. It is Dustin that notices her first in the cluster of other visitors. He nudges David on the shoulder to gather his attention to point her out. Suzanne watches them from the corner of her eye as Angela talks to Jackie about the tour and its agenda. She smiles vaguely to keep an appearance as she continues to watch the pair of men talking hurriedly to one another before turning towards the entrance of the asylum, leaving Jackie to manage the twenty guests on her own.

"Well, they are in a hurry to get started." Suzanne points this out this to Jackie in an attempt to get her moving.

"They really are," She pulls her handheld radio from her left pocket and speaks into it quickly. "Dustin, are we getting started already?" She inquires as she begins to quickly gather the remainder of the tickets and check names off of her list.

"David and I are checking a couple of things," Dustin replies in a calloused voice. "Keep them occupied until we return." He instructs in a growl that comes across as static on the radio.

"Yes, sir," Jackie responds rapidly. "We shall await your return before starting. I will have them ready." Jackie adds in an attempt to sound trustworthy and gain brownie points on her first day of the job.

"Just keep an eye on them. All of them." He responds before the radio goes silent. Jackie looks around at the group in a curious manner catching onto the hint that he means someone particular but not the least bit sure on who he means or why. Suzanne nudges Angela pointedly in the ribs as she feigns moving towards the crowd herself. Angela nods in assurance before approaching Jackie with the brochure in her hands and letting her dark hair down.

"Hey, while we are waiting," Suzanne hears Angela stammer in a loud, awkward tone. "Can you explain some of these sights to me?"

"What do you mean?" Jackie asks in a tone of utter surprise and unpreparedness.

Suzanne rushes to the first tree on the property, dipping behind it before she remembers to take a breath. Peeking around the corner, she watches as the members of the group, including Jackie, seem to go about their conversations without noticing she has disappeared. Keeping to the shadows, Suzanne lurks behind bushes and trees until she arrives at the caretaker's shed where she had made her escape on her previous visit. Retracing her steps, she enters the asylum arriving back in the maintenance office closet.

Suzanne pulls her flashlight from her back pocket as soon as she enters the shed to find her way into the tunnels. She moves swiftly but with care not to make a sound. She has her voice recorder ready in the side mesh pocket and a set of brass knuckles, for self-defense purposes only, naturally. Once she has arrived at the maintenance office closet, she dampens the light of her flashlight with a piece of colored plastic she had once used during lighting for the church productions. Using a hair band, she secures it around the tip of the flashlight so a dull purple glow is all the tool emits. Keeping silent, she moves cautiously to the door on the opposite side of the office and cracks it open only a few inches so she can peer into the hall.

The dull orange bulbs in the hall are on, giving an eerie glow in the gray stone corridor. The orange and yellow steel doors that line the hall with small windows towards the peaks red silent and still. Their levers are all down, sealing the doors closed. She crouches low in the narrow slit of the door facing to listen intently. She can not discern any sounds in the hall aside from the loudly audible impact of leaking drops hitting the stone floor in the eerie corridor. Stepping carefully into the hall, Suzanne sticks close to the wall with her flashlight held as a weapon as much as a tool while moving along the hall towards the intersection where she had found herself on the previous visit.

Once at the intersection, Suzanne places the flashlight between her thighs to free both of her hands. She reaches into her back pocket to pull a sheet of printer paper free. Unfolding the document, she looks at a rough interpretation of a map drawn from memory. Suzanne reaches into her right pocket to pull out an engraved compass to get a bearing on her location and the direction north. Taking the left passage, she grumbles internally at the prospect of following the word of someone who wanted to kill her or take Aunt Francis, a man whose soul intentions are saving his own neck. He could either be on the level and genuinely wanting to do right if for the only reason to save himself, or he could be leading her into yet another trap. She is not ready to trust him, or his word, not yet.

She arrives at a second intersection after traveling the hall for ten minutes. This intersection runs north due south with wrought iron gates for doors. Each cubby hole has a hanging cot and a toilet with a sink for a water basin. Suzanne's stomach churns when she notices the gray brick walls are stained rust-brown in places. Most are streaks but a few resemble splatter patterns. Water drips in several of the cells, landing in overrun puddles on the floor before running out into the hall from under the barred doors. Each of these doors displays three locks, all of which require a different key.

Suzanne checks her map again with definite displeasure. turning to the south, she tries to stay in the middle of the hall as far from the doors as possible. She eases past the cells the eerie silence growing. The rhythmic dripping of water is joined by the rustling of loose tin somewhere not far from her location. The crinkling and waves of the rustling tin sound much like a heavy storm coming in strong. hidden in the background, and only making itself known when the least convenient to Suzanne, she can hear the clatter of struggling chains in unison with the banging of something heavy in a sequence that Suzanne associates with her aunt cleaving through a roast before Sunday dinner. The further along the southern corridor she travels, the louder the sounds seem to get, and the closer.

Suzanne stops at the next intersection, crouching low to the floor next to a wall. As she kneels, she keeps her flashlight low and the map pressed against the wall with her left hand. The next intersection is a west due east crossroad. The lights are dim or burned out, giving very little light in the hall making it impossible to make anything out in the corridors. Even with the light from the intersecting hall in the immediate area. Suzanne places her back against the wall while squatting. Using the light in the area, she double-checks the direction Paul had directed her to take, she groans and leans her head back against the wall.

"Suzanne," The voice of Angela comes through the hands-free communications ear bud in her left ear as she contemplates her next move. "Suzanne, come through please."

"This is Suzanne." She replies while closing her eyes and trying to think.

"The larger man just came back out and canceled tonight's tour." Angela updates her on the situation taking place outside. "He said there is a safety hazard on one of the floors of the asylum."

"Call Sam and let him know what is going on," Suzanne instructs her in a low whisper. "And then sit in my car and wait for one of us to come to you."

"He also fired that Jackie woman. He said she had failed to keep all of the group together and pointed out that you were missing." Angela adds as a side note. "They know you are in there somewhere." She points out hurriedly.

"Good to know. Let Sam know all of this as well." Suzanne instructs her before taking a final look at the map before turning her flashlight back on and taking the west passage.

14.
Wednesday 00:14
(12:14 am)

Suzanne travels along the westward pass quietly with the barrage of terrific sounds clashing all around her. She keeps the flashlight pointed downwards so only a small trace of light leads her along the dark hall. The voice of Angela informing her 'They know you are in there somewhere keeps echoing in her mind. That thought gives her doubt what she is doing traveling this desolate tunnel alone in the middle of the night. She is about to turn and run back the way she had come when she hears the creaking of a metal door opening somewhere close by. Coming to a dead stop, she lifts her light unconsciously to scan the area for any movement.

Ten feet ahead, a looming figure steps from the shadows of a passageway. The figure is dressed all in black making them hard to see or determine its size. They seem to tower over Suzanne a good three feet at best with a bulky figure and a scythe in hand. Chains hang from their body, from the shoulders and arms particularly to rattle on the ground, shimmering with a silver and red light. The figure's head is shrouded in a hood, masking its face or any features. The only flesh, or absence thereof, is the figure's skeletal hands. Suzanne's legs turn to jello as she stands looking at the figure who turns to look at her before pointing a bony finger in her direction.

"You are one creepy cat, buddy," Suzanne mutters to herself as she tries to slowly back away. A slight breeze picks up, coming with the sounds of hooved horse feet rapidly growing louder. Suzanne looks around curiously for the source of the arriving horse before the neighing echoes just beside her in an open passageway. Suzanne jumps as the sound startles her greatly. Dropping her map, Suzanne instinctively turns and runs in the opposite direction with the light of her flashlight lamp rapidly moving from floor to ceiling as her arms sway in a great hurry. The clickety Clack of the hooved horse feet seems to be pursuing her as she passes the intersection heading into the eastern corridor.

The flashing lights of the dying bulbs in this corridor give brief glimpses for Suzanne to work with. Her flashlight has become of very little help in determining what is around her in the rapid heat of her retreat from the creepy ghoulish character she has hopefully left behind in the western wing of the dungeon she has discovered under the asylum. Not knowing where to go next, Suzanne keeps her eyes peeled for another corridor, taking a sharp right as soon as she comes to a four-way intersection after several minutes. Her heart is beating loudly in her ears, her chest aching and burning with every forced breath. The sounds of pursuit begin to die down several minutes after she took the first turn and sidestepped onto a set of stairs descending into the darkness behind an old, swollen wooden door to her left.

Suzanne slides the door's sliding bolt lock into place over the ring door knob. She turns to gaze down the stairs again, removing the purple filter so the entirety casts a beam down the stone stairs to illuminate a dirt floor at the end of a stone slope corridor housing the stairs.

Suzanne is shining her light down the stairs when heavy thuds and sounds of hard impacts come against the door directly behind her. She turns suddenly in surprise and anticipation of an attack giving way for her left foot to slip on the gritty stone step. As her left foot rockets downwards out from underneath her, Suzanne falls to her face as she slides and bounces down the steps with her chest and chin being jarred on each step. She struggles to catch herself on the smooth steps before she reaches the bottom. Finally managing to get her right foot to stay on a step, she uses her hands to reach out to either side of the steps to find purchase by fingertip on cold, brittle stones. Suzanne pulls herself to a sitting position on the steps while wiping blood from her lower lip.

Each breath is labored as she hugs her ribs. A sharp pain shoots through her jaw and sides, she is certain bruises of various colors are already being spread on her flesh. She can feel the bludgeoning damage in her rib cage while she sits waiting for the pain to subdue enough to continue. She can see her flashlight rolling from side to side at the bottom of the steps. The light seems to dull on the dirt floor as it shines out into the chamber outside of the arched entrance way five feet down the corridor. Adjusting her backpack on her shoulders, Suzanne climbs gingerly to her feet before descending the steps one at a time before reaching the bottom.

Suzanne crouches once she reaches the bottom landing, extending her right arm towards her flashlight while investigating the chamber. The room she looks into is small, roughly the size of a thirty by thirty room. There is a wooden chair situated towards the back of the room with restraint straps on either armrest and from the legs. A wiring harness is situated along the back of the chair leading to a metal headgear that is resting on a hook on the back of the chair. A control panel rests several feet away from the chair with a series of switches and gauges. A cup holding long, thin prongs hangs on the side of the console next to wound wires attached to scissor clamps. Suzanne can not help but imagine this device is used for sinister intentions.

Three chairs are set around the room with tables next to them covered in instruments. A camera rests on a tripod facing the ominous chair. Suzanne moves in slowly while shining her flashlight around the stone room. A bucket of tools set to the side of the chair containing a hammer, pliers, and spikes. Each has a rust discoloration splattered about them. Suzanne can only imagine where that came from. She is halfway across the room when there is another loud impact on the door at the top of the steps. She turns around abruptly to shine her flashlight on the entrance in time to feel a slight sting at the base of her neck.

Suzanne raises a hand to her neck to feel for what caused the discomfort. Her hand pulls away a small syringe dart with small green feathers. Her eyesight begins to blur as Mr. Tuttle steps out from a shadow to hover towards her. She stumbles backward as she struggles against the effect of the dart's contents. Shaking her head from side to side, she reaches for her handheld radio and tries to contact Angela.

"Angela," She calls desperately. "I am in the furthermost basement. I need help, I think they have drugged me." Suzanne stammers as she stumbles backward into the menacing chair. Her arms fall limp as she slides down into the chair. The groggy sensation she has been fighting is becoming more intense as she begins to whimper. The looming figure of Mr. Tuttle comes in and out of vision as her eyes become too heavy to hold open.

"Come in Angela," Suzanne remarks though the hand holding the radio has fallen from the arm of the chair. The radio thuds lightly on the dirt floor as she begins to drool from the corners of her mouth. "I am in serious trouble." She whispers before falling further into the wooden chair. She finally succumbs to sleep as Tuttle looms over her, the physical persona falling away as a mirage image falls to reveal a blurring vision of David working briskly to strap Suzanne's arms and legs to the chair.

When Suzanne wakes, there is a dull sting on her head. Her eyes feel puffy and swollen and her hearing is distorted. She tries to move on the hard surface only to find her body is restrained around the waist and chest. Her hands and legs are also bound to the wooden surface she clings to unwillingly. She tries to look around, uncertain of where she is or what brought her to where she is. Her memories, as foggy as her blurred vision, echo agony in her mind as she tries to think. The room is dark save a dull light that expands in her tear-filled eyes. Suzanne struggles against her restraints to no avail as a groggy-looking figure lurches into view.

"Who are you?" Suzanne requests disdainfully.

"You will not need to know in a few minutes." A familiar voice responds as they set a pole next to Suzanne. A clear IV bag hangs, swaying in the sudden movement of being relocated. Suzanne feels a slight sting in the crease of her left arm, a quick pinch followed by a prolonged instrument lingering in her arm with an adhesive being placed over to hold it in place.

"This will not be painful, but it will ruin you." The familiar voice remarks casually. "No one will know to mourn you. Your car will be seen driving through town to a seedy section of town. A letter will be found, typed out, and placed with your belongings. People will say you broke under the pressure. We all know you have been struggling. We have been keeping an eye on you since you took the case." Suzanne closes her eyes as she struggles internally to regain her vision and memories. Whatever they dosed her with is strong, very strong. Once she opens her eyes again, she can see David setting the tools and instruments in preparation for something unfavorable. Her memories come flooding back of where she is and what she set out to do.

"Do you really think your plan is going to work?" Suzanne inquires patiently. She rotates her head so that her neck pops audibly. The warm fluids entering her arm send a shiver down her spine and the dull brown room begins to illuminate with vibrant colors that move and swivel around the open room.

"It already is. We contacted the widow Tuttle again an hour ago, she is meeting Dustin in about twenty minutes." David retorts sourly as he turns to look at her. Suzanne's pupils are heavily dilated, and her head lobs gingerly from side to side as her body slouches in the chair. "The last thing I have to do is tie up loose ends."

"I'm not the only one that knows about you," Suzanne remarks groggily. In her last efforts to free herself, she begins prying her right foot out of her slip-on boot from under the rope while painfully dislocating her thumb on her right hand. "We have Paul in custody. He has been telling my brother everything." Suzanne tries to keep him engaged while working herself free.

"Paul has gotten himself free," David remarks with a chuckle. "His Lawyer got him off, free as a bird." David turns towards the sharp probes, attaching a wire to the end of them. Switching the machine on, there is an electrical hum radiating from the machine as sparks fly from where the clamp makes contact with the spike.

David turns around quickly with the spike arching down towards her leg. In a swift motion, Suzanne kicks out with her now free barefoot leg. Her kick lands in his groin, catching him by surprise. With her free hand, she grabs his gloved hand holding the spike and plunges it forcefully into his own leg. There is a moment where David's body jars and contorts before the electrical charge pulses with lightning coursing from the rod. Suzanne shuts the machine off and smiles as light smoke rises from his hair. Compelled to laugh by whatever is being inserted into her arm, Suzanne carefully removes the IV needle before unfastening her bindings.

Suzanne stumbles over to David and feels for a pulse in his wrist while laughing and giggling. She finds a faint pulse in his limp limb and breathes a sigh of relief. Pulling the cords free from the machine, she uses them to bind him tightly to the chair. Leaving her boot behind, She grabs her backpack and stumbles from the room while placing it on her shoulders. She stops for a moment and grimaces in her delusional state.

Grabbing her dislocated thumb, she uses the medical knowledge she had gotten from an old friend and rests the finger with an audible pop. She spits blood as she bites through her lower lip. Tears stream heavily from her eyes as she looks around, picking up her flashlight from a nearby table. Switching it on, she spits another loogie of blood to the floor before giggling and climbing up the steps back to the wooden door.

Suzanne clips her radio back onto her belt, placing the earpiece back into her right ear. Moving slowly, she keeps one hand on the wall in an effort to keep her balance as she struggles to walk. Her vision is still distorted, causing the room around her to spin and move, placing her off balance and struggling to push on. Moving at a slow pace, the colors of the room persist, following her from the basement to the floor of the asylum where the cells reside for the criminally insane. After several minutes of working her way through the halls, the sequences of the pulsing yellow-orange bulbs and the swirling cascade of vibrant colors become overwhelming. Suzanne places her back against the wall of the hall and slides down to sit with her knees to her chest.

"Angela," Suzanne remarks into the radio. "I need you and Sam." She whispers fleetingly. " I am in the underground ward. They have me dosed with something. I am really struggling." She waits several minutes with no response, only static. digging in her back pocket, she pulls out her cellphone. With her vision distorted, she can not see the screen well enough to dial or use any of the functions. Letting her arm drop, she leans against the wall with a heavy feeling of defeat and failure.

"Suzanne!" Sam's voice comes across the radio in her earpiece. "Where are you?"

15.

Wednesday 05:12

(5:12 am)

"Sam, is that you?" Suzanne asks with a strong sense of relief expanding from her as she crouches against the wall.

"Yeah, I am in the parking lot of the asylum. Your car is the only one on the lot." Sam replies calmly. "Where are you?"

"I am in the bottom cell ward, one floor down from the ground floor," Suzanne informs him quickly. "They dosed me with something. Some sort of hallucinogens. "I think I have David tied fairly well in the basement, but Dustin is scheduled to meet Mrs. Tuttle for the payout in an hour. You need to get to her." Suzanne stammers as she continues to try and look around the hall with her vision still too blurred and distorted for her to move. The entire area is moving and spinning in her vision, making her disoriented and unable to move.

"I will come to get you and then we will go intervene." Sam offers quickly.

Suzanne can hear his car door opening as he speaks.

"No," Suzanne counters sternly. "Angela is still here somewhere. She can help me, you go catch Dustin at the drop point." She instructs firmly. "I'll be okay."

"Are you sure, Suzanne?" Sam insists. "I can get you quickly and we can go stop them together."

"No, go on," Suzanne instructs again. "Angela will help me."

"Alright, Sis," Sam replies, closing his door again. "I will get ahold of Mrs. Tuttle and stop the transaction. Then, I am coming right back here."

"Okay. Be careful." Suzanne warns before closing her eyes once more and sitting quietly against the cold stone wall. Her body feels tingly and weak. Her stomach churns from consistent motion sickness. Suzanne keeps her eyes closed, but climbs carefully to her feet while sliding up the wall. Using the radio, she tries once more to contact Angela.

"Angela, where are you?" She calls out desperately into the radio and quiet void of space.

"I am coming, Suzanne." Comes the much-needed reply. "I just escaped an attacker, I am on my way."

"I need your help," Suzanne calls out to her. She slides along the wall, feeling with her trembling hands. In her distorted vision, the shadows of the corridor slowly take over where the lights from the orbs along the wall transform from a yellow glow to a mirage of flying creatures similar to bats or dark birds. Suzanne groans anxiously while still wiping her eyes which are steadily becoming raw. Any sounds in the corridor are muffled in her delusional state, keeping her from hearing the steady approach of a silent figure coming from the shadows behind her.

"Angela, where are you?" Suzanne asks again in a low frantic whisper. The figure behind her continues to close the distance between them and Suzanne, coming up behind her in a long black cloak with the hood pulled up over their head. The figure slowly raises a steel pipe in their delicate hands.

"I am right here," Suzanne hears Angela reply from close by. Suzanne turns just in time to see a long piece of bludgeoning weapon come sweeping down at her. The steel pipe strikes her on the shoulder between her neck and her collar bone, pushing her to the ground painfully. Suzanne falls to her back with the corridor swirling around her in vibrant colors with a mass of shadowy bats. The figure approaches, standing over top of her with the pipe held high over their head.

Suzanne kicks out hard with both feet, only the left finding any purchase on the cloaked figure who stumbles from the attack. Suzanne rolls painfully to her side and frantically begins climbing to her feet while stumbling from one side of the hall to the other. As she stumbles forward hunched over, there is a sharp pain as the long steel pipe makes contact along her spine sending her to the floor again. Her backpack falls aside, sliding along the floor. Suzanne cries out in great pain and anguish. using her elbows, she begins pulling herself along the floor in hopes of putting distance between her attacker and herself. Suzanne roles to her throbbing back as the figure plunges the tip of the pipe towards her.

There is a clang of metal on stone as the end of the pipe pierces clear through the fatty tissue of her ribs. Suzanne gasps and cries out wide-eyed while grasping the pipe in her hands. With a hard kick, she lunges her right foot upwards, catching the figure fully under the chin. The figure stumbles back swearing before falling to the floor.

Suzanne pulls the pipe free from her side, using it as a crutch to pull herself from the floor to her feet. She turns on the spot to see the figure sitting up from a prone position. The hood of the cloak falls back to reveal Angela looking up at her. Suzanne takes several steps back while looking down at her friend in a swirling mass of vibrant colors and swirling bats. Angela climbs to her feet drawing a bowie knife from beneath her cloak. She lunges at Suzanne with malice in her eyes. As she draws the weapon over her head, blade down, Suzanne stumbles to her right and swings the steel pipe at eye level. The pipe collides with the side of Angela's temple causing her to spin in place. Her knife clangs to the floor as she falls unconscious at Suzanne's feet.

"I will never understand what I do to people to make them turn on me," Suzanne mutters as she grabs Angela's ankle. Stumbling and fighting against the effect of the drug in her system, she drags Angela to one of the padded cells. Pushing the switch up, she opens the cell door and drags Angela inside. Suzanne props her against the far wall before stumbling out. Her vision is still distorted, causing the task at hand to take much longer than it normally would. Suzanne is about to leave when Angela begins to stir back to consciousness. Suzanne quickly limps out of the room and slams the door shut just as Angela climbs to her feet and lunges towards the opening.

"Let me out of here, Suzanne, and I will let you walk away unhurt," Angela screams through the thin pane of glass that makes up the small window. A hinged slot in the door opens as her hand slides through in an attempt to grab Suzanne.

"Too late for that, Angela." Suzanne remarks as she slides down the wall a few feet away. Coming to rest on the floor with her back to the wall, Suzanne closes her eyes while fighting the sensation to vomit. "Want to tell me why you did all of this?" She inquires impatiently while gagging between phrases.

"Let me out!" Angela screams fanatically.

"Sam will when he gets here," Suzanne replies cautiously. "In the meantime, anything you tell me may help your case." She offers softly. She keeps her eyes closed while laying her head against the wall in hopes of allowing the effects to wear off in time.

"You will be too late," Angela yells while slamming against the padded door. "Dustin will have received the payoff from my grandmother and skipped town."

"So Mrs. Tuttle is your grandmother," Suzanne smiles with victory. "I assume you have been removed from the will? Or possibly disowned?"

"All because I did a stint in prison for a felony theft charge." Angela curses and slams the door again. "See, it is just justice being served to an elderly, stingy woman."

Suzanne thinks back recalling a case she had worked on for Brandon a few years back. An Angela Watters had been arrested for grand larceny, and Brandon had been the prosecuting attorney on the case. Now that she thinks about it, she recalls seeing Mrs. Tuttle in the audience behind the defendant's seat. Angela had been charged for grand larceny of a car belonging to a council member of Darlington County, the son of the Mayor. They had given her twenty years at the time with no chance of parole.

"How did you get out of prison?" Suzanne asks curiously.

"My people outside of the prison paid a guard off. That helped me pass through the soiled laundry and make my escape." Angela explains sourly. "I won't go back."

"I am sorry to tell you, you may have no other option." Suzanne remarks as she resituates on the floor. She still keeps her eyes close, allowing her stomach to settle and her nerves to ease down. Resting for a little bit, she can feel herself regaining some strength and balance despite the battle of the substance they put in her.

"What did you dose me with?" Suzanne inquires, still slightly uneasy.

"A powerful hallucinogen and sedative combination. It was meant to place you in a comma." Angela snarls.

"We will just wait here for Sam to return," Suzanne remarks groggily. She shifts positions again before falling unconscious where she sits.

Suzanne wakes to find Sam shaking her awake. A paramedic is kneeling beside her with an IV bag held aloft in her right hand while clear fluids run steadily along the clear lines into her arm. Several syringes rest on a cloth beside her. Several officers are removing Angela from the cell in cuffs as she fights against them violently. The swirling colors and distorting still linger in her vision, though subtly wearing down. The paramedics are beginning to ease her onto a gurney while Sam silently gives out instructions. Suzanne reaches toward her ears, curious as to why she can not hear. To her dismay, her arms, legs, and torso have been restrained. She looks at the female paramedic while two males begin moving her.

"I can't hear," Suzanne yells though incapable of hearing her own voice.

The female paramedic places a cool cloth against her forehead and purses her lips together as if softly and kindly making a noise of comfort. Suzanne contently closes her eyes again and allows herself to drift back to sleep despite the desire to know what is going on. When she wakes a final time, she is in her usual room at Darlington County General where her name is engraved on a placard on the door. Sam and Dean wait in chairs against the wall while Aunt Francis sits in a more comfortable lounge chair beside Suzanne's bed. Alannia, Jerry, and Hannah sit close by on the opposite side of the bed with Bee and Wilson standing at the foot. Suzanne instantly reaches for her forehead, the throbbing in her dome more than she has ever experienced. Dean is the first to notice her movement. He nudges Sam before rushing over to the bed and sitting on the edge.

"I'm glad you are finally awake, Suzanne." Dean remarks with a broad smile.

"Shame on you for giving us such a scare, Suzanne." Jerry teases with a chuckle of relief.

"I am not so sure I want to be awake with my head hurting like this," Suzanne retorts quietly.

"You alright, sis?" Sam inquires from the other side of the bed.

"Just feel like my head has been trampled," Suzanne remarks quietly. "What happened once I lost the fight to stay awake?"

"You caught Angela, which is a big win. Dustin is in custody. We caught up to Mrs. Tuttle before she could make the drop." Sam explains in a low voice. "We found you unconscious by the door to the cell where you trapped her. The paramedics had to work with you for several minutes to stabilize you before they could move you. You went through quite an ordeal in the basement and lower chamber."

"They drugged me with something." Suzanne retorts.

"Yeah, pretty strong too," Sam remarks. "But we managed to get David to talk and counteract the effects."

"I'm glad you did." Suzanne yawns, suddenly very tired. "I never felt worse in my life."

"Well, Angela was Mrs. Tuttle's granddaughter who was upset about being taken from the will after committing a felony. She and her friends created the plot to scare Mrs. Tuttle with the projection of her late husband." Sam Explains.

"Yeah, with the knowledge of her grandparent's home, she was able to set the projectors, come and go with a spare key, and use her memories of her grandfather to manipulate her grandmother," Suzanne adds before laying back on her pillows. The lights in the room are dulled considerably which is a help to Suzanne in a large way. "Paul, her naive boyfriend, helped her begin her plans before helping her break free of prison."

"You solved another one, Suzanne," Dean remarks proudly while squeezing her hand. "Mrs. Tuttle gave me an envelope for you. It is in my duffle bag." He adds before leaning over and giving her a kiss.

"It will help to finish my house." Suzanne remarks with a broad smile.

"It is more than enough with some left over to finish paying for the restoral of your home, sis," Sam assures her proudly. "Get some rest and we will be here when you wake again."

Jerry approaches her side, Hannah's right hand in his left, and leans over to kiss Suzanne's forehead gently. She smiles with an ease of comfort.

"I love you, Suzanne." He whispers softly just by her ear.

"I love you, daddy." She remarks before dozing back off.

William L. Jeffers

Please feel free to email me at jeffersarchivefoundry@gmail.com or visit me at www.facebook.com/jeffersarchives www.jeffersarchivefoundry.blogspot.com for exclusive content, chapter previews, or new on current and future novels.

I am a member of the Apple Grove, Ashton, and Glenwood areas of Mason County, West Virginia where I attended and graduated from Hannan High School. My family and I attend morning services at Fairfield Church. I am a husband, father, uncle, son, brother, and soon to be poppy. I treasure time with my family, life on my small farm, the God given ability to write and share my stories with others such as you, and enjoy small entertainments. Aside from the Sturgeon's mysteries, I write gothic mystery, epic fantasy, and horror/suspense. Though, I have been known to write romantic drama and a comedy.

9 798373 807623